THIS UNUSUAL LIFE

JAMIE SANDS

Grey Kelpie Studio

This Unusual Life!

ISBN kindle edition 978-0-473-57709-4

Paperback 978-0-473-57707-0

Epub 978-0-473-57708-7

Published by Grey Kelpie Studio

Dedicated to Ellen "we could get an onion!" Boucher

LETTER TO THE PUBLISHING HOUSE

Dear Mx Sands,

Grey Kelpie Studio

Please find attached the manuscript I told you about over the phone.

Welcome to this rather unusual (if you will forgive the terminology in this particular instance) book. This is one of those 'found art' pieces, and I hope that you will find it enlightening. But first, indulge me in laying out some context before you read the strange and at times alarming material I have included in this collection.

I live in Auckland, New Zealand, which is a small country in the South Pacific. Our country is a democracy and a Monarchy, under Queen Elizabeth the Second's Commonwealth, but with a local elected Prime Minister. I mention this only because I want to make explicit that the queen and the royal family mentioned in this book are definitely not our Queen or royal family and I don't wish to get into any trouble.

Recently, I was lucky enough to purchase a house. It's a new build in a moderately priced subdivision rather far from town. Myself and my spouse are the first to own this particular house, and we moved in three days after construction had completed. The house is one of many identical looking things, but we like it very much. The area that the subdivision is built on was previously farm-land and before that, some hundred years earlier, native forest of the kind with tree ferns and densely packed trees.

About a week after we'd moved in, In the process of unpacking our things, I decided to keep the moving boxes, in a broken down format, and store them in our attic. I went up there and discovered something quite strange.

Our attic wasn't empty, in fact it looked like the attic of a house that had stood for some time. There was a thick layer of dust and an old dress form, a half-completed ball gown still pinned to it. The style of the dress evoked something from the 1950s, with a cinched waist and flared skirt. There were some boxes of old books - Reader's Digest compilations, old Western cowboy novels and some Mills and Boon romances. None of the books or magazines had a publication date later than 1961. But the most extraordinary discovery is what led to the creation of this book.

I stumbled upon a shoebox of clippings in the attic. They appear to be clippings from a year or so's run of a magazine. The shoebox had a faded inscription on it reading "This Unusual Life! Highlights" and inside was the selection of clippings that I have collected for you here. There were a couple of pieces of ephemera in the box as well, a pink ballpoint pen with no ink left in it, a ticket stub to a movie called "The Farthing Moor" and some dried rose petals.

Once you have read through the selection of clippings I'm sure you'll agree that they seem to evoke something quite unworldly. I have done research of my own, enquiring in the United Kingdom and locally, as well as in Australia and some other English-speaking countries of the Commonwealth, but there is no record of any publication called This Unusual Life!

I have also not been able to find any record of any of the locations mentioned or the specific people.

You may notice, as you read, some familiar brand names and celebrities, but while familiar, one can assume it is not the same as the ones you and I are familiar with in our world based on their actions. I have made a few notes throughout the collection in brackets and with italics. I have tried to keep these sparse so as to not draw attention away from the writings.

I hope that you enjoy this collection as much as I enjoyed reading and collating them. I have little notion that I've provided them in the right order or as the original magazine editor would have chosen, but I have done my best to ensure some sort of sense.

Please let me know if you have any additions or edits you'd like to make.

Thank you so much for this opportunity,

[name redacted by Publisher]

Publisher's note:

Grey Kelpie Studio have chosen to go forward with the publishing of this charming collection despite the disappearance of the author who compiled it. All proceeds will go to their spouse to aid in the campaign to find them.

THIS UNUSUAL LIFE!

THIS UNUSUAL LIFE!

(Editor's note: Found topmost in the shoebox of clippings, this intro piece from what looks like an inside cover of the magazine.

A magazine for the strange, modern world we find ourselves in. Whether you're a stay-at-home dad, a mother on the go, a singleton or living in a polyamorous commune with the members of your blood cult, This Unusual Life! is the magazine for you.

APRIL 1955

NEAR DEATH EXPERIENCE THWARTED BY FAMILY VAMPIRE

A YOUNG LOCAL woman diced with death recently when a home invader surprised her one night. Alice, 23, was alone in her West Goldmarsh house, enjoying a cosy night of Netflix and Quill, which as we all know involves watching Netflix as you consume bread rolls shaped like hedgehogs, when the invasion happened.

Alice had planned a peaceful night in. The young schoolteacher, known to her community as a warm, happy grasslady, is often to be found at home on weeknights. Police speculate this knowledge was useful to the intruder.

"I didn't know what to do," Alice said. "One moment I was chilling with my breadhogs and then next there was this woman there with a knife to my throat. I froze up, this was just like the case my true crime podcast covered the other week, but in that one, they had killed the poor soul. I didn't want to be a victim!"

For a tense moment it did look like she would be the victim. "My attacker was behind me, so it was hard to see who or what it was, but I definitely got the feeling it was an older, white woman," she said. "You know, the kind of person who would ask for the manager over something like a missing packet of free ketchup."

It was then that her terrifying ordeal became something out of a movie. "There was a noise upstairs, and I thought that was strange because I typically prefer to live alone, but then Count Vanya came down the stairs and I thought, I've never been happier to see my uncle, never been happier that he dropped in unannounced. He swooped right across the room and bit the intruder in the neck. He also took her outside and I don't know what he did then, but there was no body," Alice said.

Count Vanya, Alice's Uncle, lives with the frightening but ultimately misunderstood condition of vampirism. Vampirism affects roughly one in twenty and manifests as a horrifying transfiguration of the body into one of the undead. It's also accompanied by a curse that makes the diseased individual crave the living blood and flesh of unaffected people. Some say one of the symptoms of the disease is to make the infected stronger and more resilient, but these claims are not proven by scientific research. Vampirism infected individuals tend to avoid densely populated areas, since the "Vampire hunts" of the late sixties and the following "Undead rights movement" failed to gain much traction.

Alice's Uncle Vanya, she reports, lives abroad much of the year, and only attends family gatherings such as births, will readings and marriages. "It was just dumb luck he was there," Alice said. "He must've known my sister was about to give birth. After the incident, we had a really nice baby shower and he gave the new baby a teddy bear. It's a really high quality one as well, not one of those cheap Kmart stuffed toys."

Alice's sister, Annabeth, was quick to shut down any speculation that it was unsafe to have a vampire near her newborn child. "You should have seen him with the baby, it was very sweet. He was so gentle. He was doing this thing where he waved the teddy bear at the baby and made a little growly noise. The baby loved it, just giggled and gurgled the whole time. Couldn't take their eyes off him."

Although little is known about who the intruder was, or the purpose for the invasion, Alice doesn't feel afraid in her neighbourhood. "Uncle Vanya has agreed to stay with me for a while," she says. Smiling, she continues. "It was a terrifying ordeal, but ultimately, it brought my family closer together."

Alice is bravely returning to watching Netflix tonight, after taking what she calls "a couple of days off".

Uncle Vanya was unavailable for comment.

If you want to enjoy Netflix and Quill, check page 43 for Alice's hedgehog shaped bread roll recipe! You'll literally die from cuteness.

- Peachy Buncheeks reporting

BYTOWN PORTRAIT ATTACKS

a special This Unusual Life! report

A CHILLING REPORT from Bytown this week - a number of family portraits have been vandalised by a gang with an unknown motivation.

Several Bytown families were hit in what seems to have been an organised and calculated spate of attacks. Each time the gang waited until the family was out of the house and the coast was clear. Then evidence shows they either broke in or used a spare key to gain access to the house.

Once inside, nothing was stolen or removed from the premises, but family portraits have been defaced and destroyed. Several families report knife slashes across the faces, particularly the eyes, whereas some others have been completely painted over with black or red spray-paint.

"It was truly chilling," Montemarte Finesse said, in a tearful interview. She clutched a large, framed portrait taken at her local mall. The faces have all been scribbled over with permanent marker, but the photo appears to be of her, her spouse and their two children, all wearing matching white shirts and blue jeans. "We came back in and the door was ajar, I immediately thought the worst. My jewellery and cash were all still lying around on the kitchen floor, like always, so I was reassured, up until I saw this."

We paused while Montemarte dabbed at her eyes. "It was such a special day, we'd gone to so much trouble to find clothes that matched, the photographer was so charismatic, and the experience was lovely. Then after we did the photoshoot, we got bubble tea."

The Finesse family was one of dozens affected. At the time of publishing there's been no solid witness accounts or any explanation for what the gang's intention is with this ruthless destruction of family portraiture.

If you or anyone you know has any information, please come forward and let us know.

- Tiger Smith reporting

PRINCE LARKSPUR STEPS OUT WITH MYSTERY WOMAN

SOCIAL MEDIA and the rumour mill worked overtime last night after several pictures were shared of The Nation's favourite playboy Prince Larkspur out on the town with what many are speculating is his new girlfriend. The pair were seen leaving popular night club Whatsit, and many report that the prince's hand kept on touching her body. Both are all smiles in the photos taken. Nothing is known about this woman, beyond that she is a brunette with very straight teeth.

Prince Larkspur is the eldest child of Her Venerable Majesty Queen Laurel (may She ever rule these lands), for several centuries now he has captured the hearts of The Nation. Sometimes literally, for example in the hunts the royal family used to embark upon in the nineteenth century. Many a young lass and lad was blessed enough to die on his knife and subsequently had their hearts take pride of place in the National Museum to the Royal Family.

With his charming smile, full to the brim with so many delicately pointed teeth, his dark curled hair and his gorgeously tanned skin, he has always been The Nation's sweetheart.

Prince Larkspur has kept gossip columnists busy with this string of ill-fated love affairs.

Although many, including rival magazine *These Days*, thought he'd found his true match with Prince Forest of the Summer Court, this reporter could tell the two were never meant to be. That didn't stop endless speculations on their wedding, the likelihood of them having children and whether or not they were sharing clothing.

The curse on poor Prince Forest tore them apart in April last year, as we all knew it would. Since then, Prince Larkspur has had a series of dates with different folk, but nothing any royal would call serious. He has a large, dedicated Fanclub who often appear at his scheduled appearances with signs saying things like "Bite me, Prince Larkspur" and "Your next spouse is right here." This news could be a big disappointment to his loyal fans if the rumours are true.

Prince Larkspur's troubled love life could be changing as witnesses from the club report that the prince and the mystery woman danced and drank together all night. Photos confirm they left in the same car and one can assume that their night didn't end there. Stay tuned, as we'll be watching this story closely and reporting any updates as quickly as we can.

This Unusual Life!'s retrospective on Prince Larkspur's previous affairs is on page 13

- Cedric Ramekin reporting

QUESTION CRESSIDA

Introducing: Our new advice column!

CRESSIDA HAS PREVIOUSLY WORKED for the Daily News, Monsters of Slime-town and in a small temple on the edge of the mountains of Direwold. Here's a little from Cressida in her own words.

Hi everyone! I'm really excited to be bringing my knowledge of the world behind the veil, the spirits from beyond the grave and the small mice that live under my letterbox to you all. I truly hope I can be of some help, especially with that recipe that you just can't quite seem to master.

Please get in touch immediately with any question that has been troubling you, and I shall consult all the tools at my disposal to bring you the best, most true answer.

🦟

This Unusual Life! would love to connect you with Cressida. Please write in with your questions using email, sky writing, passenger pigeon or delivery hog, and Cressida will respond in an upcoming issue.

Question from Babbit Mistlethrush: What is the cause of the winds, and whence do they come, and whither do they go?

My dear Babbit,

Although none can be truly sure of where or what the wind's cause is, many believe it is due to the precipitation of trees on the mountains. Indeed, some say it has something to do with the flapping of a butterfly's wings as it winters in Borneo. However, I sense the true meaning behind your question, and I wish to address it directly.

There are none who have taken your spectacles. You were not robbed or played for a fool. Instead, they have simply slipped down the side of the couch where you are wont to sit, and should you stick your hand very far down (even where there are gross crumbs) you'll find them again.

Thanks for getting in touch Babbit, I hope when the winds come for you, they will treat you with kindness.

My husband of six years unexpectedly underwent an evolution and is now a tiger. We're both quite surprised by this but he's enjoying it immensely and I love him just as he is. However, this will mean some adjustments to our lives. How do we deal with our landlord who insists he now counts as a "pet", and also get his workplace to understand that the occasional devouring of coworkers is just part of his nature? Elle Izard

Dear Elle,

First of all, let me congratulate your husband on his evolution and commend you for adjusting so easily to this super important life event. As with so many things, you just need time to sort out these ills. The landlord can be reminded of the WereCreature Housing Amendment Act of 1965, although it doesn't sound like your husband is were per se, the act should cover any concerns your landlord has.

In terms of his workplace, again they just need to see that he can still do the job the same as he always could. With your support, he will get through this difficult time of transition and come out the other side brighter, happier and more sure of himself.

I would also advise that the both of you consider building a large ornamental pond in the backyard, as tigers love to swim and the pond will have the added benefit of attracting local wildlife such as small children and providing sanctuary for insects of all kinds.

Cressida, are you my aunt? I mean, really?

My darling, what is an aunt if not someone who cares for you? So yes, I am really your aunt. I'm sorry my birthday card was late, but I will make it up to you. Come and stay with me and I'll take you out for dinner, sweetheart. Do you still like Japanese food best? I'll bring you to the nicest little yakitori bar and we can talk about what's bothering you. No judgement, just love and advice if you need it.

My partner discovered our teenagers' stash of weed. How much can we steal before they notice?
From Anonymous polyamorous parents of 5 teenagers.

Dear Anonymous,

As with any theft, the key to remaining undetected isn't necessarily the action itself but the circumstances around the moment of the theft. While some might say a small fire or explosion is too extreme a distraction, I've often found that in the right place and at the right time it's exactly the thing.

Once you have a safe location for your fire or distraction, one of you can set it off (I suggest Bobby for this task) and lure the teenager towards it. Then another of you (Perhaps Glorp? She's been doing so well with her Pilates) can rappel down from the ceiling and help yourself to their stash while your husband Mizumo hacks into the system of security cameras and reports to your girlfriend and boyfriend (Teacup and Strudel) who will of course be ready with the getaway vehicles.

I would urge you, however, to consider talking to your teenager about whether they would rather be the target of a heist, or if they would like to contribute to the team's efforts. Perhaps as a united family unit you could steal more and bigger things, while strengthening the bond between you all.

Dear Cressida, Please, I need your help. How can I tell if my dog and cat are plotting against me? Prunella Bunce

It is a truth universally acknowledged that a person in possession of both a dog and a cat must be in want of plotting. In short, they absolutely are, but I think you knew that already dearest Prunella.

The real trouble you will see in the near future does not come from your pets however, it's about the weeds in the far left corner of your garden. They are beginning to gain sentience and will need organising very soon. If left uninterrupted they may start to prey on birds and other small animals. In order to avoid this, please gently guide them to salvage scraps from your compost heap. This will soon prove a robust symbiotic ecosystem for the new plant society and yourself.

HOROSCOPES

ARIES

There's no way to stop you. If you decide you're going to run, no one will stop you running. You run, son, run and run and run. The sun is fun.

Taurus

You would've liked it if they'd brought you the cherry tomatoes that the menu said was included in the meal. You really like cherry tomatoes, and the dish was fine without it. Fine. But cherry tomatoes would have been perfection.

Gemini

Some nights you're the crocodile. Some nights you're the notebook. Sometimes there's a tiny crocodile living in your leg. It's fine, it doesn't want to come out. Just feed it with fish every now and then you'll be fine.

Cancer

The thing you've been looking forward to may or may not happen. Be careful to pay attention to the world around you. Your relationship may be strong, or it may be facing some changes.

Leo

The choir that's following you around will, endlessly. There's nothing you can do to dissuade them. But in time, they will start singing the songs you like. You just have to supply them with a song list. Hang in there, Leo!

Virgo

2, 7, 24, 65

Libra

You are strongest when you're leading others, but the true strength in yourself is letting yourself be led. The leading leads the led, and the leaders are led by leading.

Scorpio

Time to shine, Scorpio. The planets are aligned, the genders are in flux, the bells ring only for thee. Get out there now! You got this!

Sagittarius

Your podcast idea has some merit, maybe it is worth recording a bit, but it'd probably be better if you got live guests on. And then maybe get them to perpetrate crimes as you record them. There's a lot of money in true crime podcasts, time to cash in on that market.

Capricorn

You will get what you need. Everyone gets what they need, in the end.

. . .

Aquarius

The ocean sings to you in the night. Do not deny the call of the ocean. It has so many things to show you. Go and learn.

Pisces

Secret spider babies. It's probably not something you can avoid, so prepare now. The secret spider babies are coming in the next Mercury Retrograde.

QUIZ!

Which cryptid is your perfect personality match?

FIRST UP, my ideal pet would be:
   A: a cute, cuddly dog
   B: a shaggy goat
   C: 7 (seven) spiders
   D: a small round rock with a shiny under side

What do you wear on the weekends?
   A is for Athleisure wear, workout gear for the win!
   B: Blanket and PJs, weekends are for blobbing
   C: whatever is Clean, but something with some fluff is ideal
   D: A carpet, so no one can see me, Dawg

Choose the best ice cream flavour:
   A Vanilla
   B: Cookies and cream
   C: Screams of the innocents
   D: Roadkill surprise with a caramel swirl

· · ·

What is your number one, must-have food item?
  A: Kale smoothie
  B: Pizza
  C: Tacos
  D: Chocolate chip cookies

What did you deliver last?
  A: someone's lunch, I moonlight as a food delivery driver
  B: A bone-chilling shriek
  C: Some twigs and bits of old bones into a friend's letterbox
  D: A mountain goat's baby

RESULTS!

Mostly A

If you picked mostly A answers then your personality match is Mothman! That's right, the spooky man moth hybrid who sometimes warns people of danger and sometimes causes the problem. Just like you! You might find it hard to keep a relationship with your glowing red eyes, but hang in there mothpeople, we know the right person is out there for you somewhere. You just keep running around the countryside and being an omen, and things will work out.

Mostly B

You already knew this, but you're a chupacabra! Kinda edgy, a bit goth or punk, and definitely down to sneak around at night and spook some farmers. Your friends know that you're the one to call if they have a problem that needs solving. But you need to look after yourself first, chupacabra. Make sure you're meeting your own needs, eating enough, drinking plenty of blood and resting. Remember, you must secure your own oxycontin mask before you help with someone else's.

· · ·

Mostly C

You're a swamp monster, you lucky thing! You could be a goblin, a bunyip or a hag, the exact definition is up to you. But the important thing is that you live somewhere damp, you like creepy things like tacos and fluffy blankets and you're so quirky you're known as the "Phoebe" in your group of friends. You need to remember though, that not everyone can see the real you under the quirk. Your friends need you to be sincere sometimes, and a neat bit of moss isn't always a good substitute for human connection.

Mostly D

Congrats! You're a Bigfoot. Also called Yeti's, abominable snowmen and Doug from down the road, big feet have a reputation for being shy, hiding from company and using psychic powers to contact lost wanderers. Your introverted nature can cause you to withdraw from relationships, so please remember that you do need human companionship at least two months out of the year. You know who is trustworthy, it's okay to trust them with your truth.

MAY 1956

BYTOWN PORTRAIT ATTACKS

a special This Unusual Life! report follow up

WE PREVIOUSLY REPORTED the bizarre and senseless attacks on family portraiture.

This Unusual Life! is pleased to be able to report we have a follow-up. One eagle-eyed reader wrote in to reveal that all the portraits were taken in the same mall. The Bytown Family most recently affected - the Santa-Bahamas family, had posed for their portrait at the Bytown City Mall just a week before the attack.

"We'd planned it for a few days," Michaelmas Santa-Bahamas said when we called them. "Screamy had organised coordinating dungarees and checked shirts for us all. My teenage child Ravyn was really annoyed, but they put the outfit on all the same. It was a great picture. We had it in the foyer of our house. It was the envy of the cul-de-sac."

However, the prized picture was soon vandalised by the unknown hooligans who have now struck seventeen different Bytown family portraits.

The Bytown City Mall has declined to comment on the connection between these crimes, but This Unusual Life! is determined to get to the bottom of this bizarre crime spree.

The portrait was found with decoupage over each of the family's faces. The collage consisted of various images of celebrities featured in recent Oscar Best Picture winning movies, along with red roses and black suit jackets. Police have thus far refused to comment on the meaning of these images in the vandalistic decoupage.

This Unusual Life! warns our loyal readers to be wary of the Bytown City Mall portrait service, as although there's no indication they were responsible (yet), the connection is obvious. Be safe out there, folks, and we'll bring you the news on this horrendous series of crimes as soon as we have it.

- Tiger Smith reporting

※

LARKSPUR'S MYSTERY LADY REVEALED!

PREVIOUSLY WE REPORTED on Prince Larkspur's wild night at Club Whatsit with a mysterious and beautiful woman.

In an exclusive, This Unusual Life! can reveal that this lovely lady is none other than Holly Albert, a half fey, half human student of Rocksbridge university. Sources close to Ms Albert reveal that she is currently studying for a Bachelor of Business, focusing on the History of Fey Culture and Economics.

Although one can only assume that Her Venerable Majesty Queen Laurel (may She ever rule these lands) would prefer that Prince Larkspur be dating a pure blooded fey. Many royal watchers speculate that this union will not last long, due to the Queen's (may She ever rule these lands) apparent coldness to the young lady.

A student who attends many of Ms Albert's classes was available to speak to us, although wished to remain anonymous. We asked about her nature.

"She's just lovely," our source said. "She's always smiling, has a nice word for anyone. She did a really solid presentation on the potato blight the fey were wrongly accused of bringing over to our world from The Underhill. It was moving, people were in tears, and this is usually a pretty dry class. She always has really good outfits as well. Even during exam week, she never turns up in her pyjamas or with her hair messy, like the rest of us. I think it's her fey blood, it means she just doesn't get as messy as the rest of us."

Many are speculating on what it means that playboy Prince Larkspur, heartthrob of The Nation, is dating a mixed-race woman. "Maybe it just means that they like each other," royal watcher Celestine MacCarthy mused. But This Unusual Life! wonders if perhaps the ever-outrageous prince is making a statement about equal rights.

As we all know, halfblooded fey/humans are often discriminated against. The latest salary survey conducted through the Duke Oleander University shows statistics that on average, a half fey worker will receive 75% of the salary paid to a fey worker doing the same job. A human worker in the same position earns about 86% of what the fey would earn. Poverty and incarceration rates are much higher for the partially fey part of the population and there's even cases of students being turned away from schools.

Whatever the reasons, it seems Prince Larkspur is making a statement, and one wonders what Her most Illustrious Majesty Queen Laurel (may She ever rule our lands) has to say about it.

Turn to page 3 for all the collected pictures of Larkspur and Ms Albert (editor's note: the pictures were not included in the shoebox)

- Cedric Ramekin reporting

🐝

DUNGEONS AND DRAGONS

Just harmless fun or dangerous sorcery?

DUNGEONS AND DRAGONS is having a worldwide resurgence. Originally written in the seventies, and enjoying a heyday in the eighties, the game is now back. Geek is cool and D&D has even been featured in popular TV shows like Stranger Things, Sex and the Village and The Bachelorette in Literal Hell. Delving into this phenomenon is feature editor Alex Balex.

Finding your own group can be a challenge, how do you find the right people to try out D&D with?

- Many potential gamers have had a lot of luck using a food box service to match them with games looking for new players
- Alternatively, there are bulletin boards for nerds who like to game, try dialling into a 1989 era board and find some like-minded people there
- Fly a purple bird shaped kite out the front of your house. This is a universal signal which means "looking for a D&D group"

Now that you have a group, it's time to get stuck in and start to play. You'll get to invent a character, which you will be embodying during the game sessions. It's important to make a character with traits that resonate with you, and make sure you decide what they look like, how they dress and what they eat for breakfast. These details will be essential as the game goes on. Here's some helpful prompts for making your character really come to life.

- Write a backstory for your character, who were they as a child? When did they first bake a cake, and what flavour was it?
- When picking activewear, what colours are they likely to gravitate towards?
- How many mice do they keep in their shoes?
- What colour bird kite do they fly out the front of their castle/cottage/hovel/tent?

Remember if you wake up one morning, look in the mirror and see your D&D character staring back at you, you're doing it right!

Once you have the right character, a good backstory and of course your group, it can be tough to establish trust with them. For example, if you want to really level up and have your group invite you to their demon worshipping rituals outside of game night you need to show that you are worthy. Worthy of both trusting and participating in blood rituals under the new moon. There are lots of ways you can casually open the communication pathways to a deeper relationship with your gaming buddies.

- Casually mention that your goat has begun speaking to you in a human voice
- Ask the group over to your house for a potluck dinner, and serve a Victoria sponge - this is a great code that they'll understand immediately
- Fly an orange bird shaped kite off the back of your car. This a universal signal your group will understand means "I'm ready to learn the real magic."

Remember that you might not find the right group for you right away, and that's okay. Breaking up with your D&D group doesn't have to be hard. Just make them some origami birds in rainbow colours and deliver a bird to each player in the dead of night.

They'll understand.

Best of luck in your new endeavour as a D&D player, we know you'll enjoy the creative expression, the Satanic rituals and the new friendships you'll build.

- Alex Balex reporting

PRINCE FOREST'S WILD WEEKEND

PRINCE FOREST of the Summer Court seems to be taking the news that his ex, Prince Larkspur, has a new love interest rather poorly.

As we know, Prince Forest is the handsome victim of a terrible curse that prevents him from finding True Love. Multiple sources contacted us to report his gallivanting around town. Here's the time-line as best we were able to piece together.

Friday 4pm: Drinks at Club Whatsit

Friday 6pm: stalking the streets with his full antlers out, howling at passers-by, baring his teeth and showing his terrible claws while branches pushed their way out of the asphalt behind him creating a charming inner-city forest.

Friday 9.25pm: dinner at Harvest Bistro, with several friends.

Friday 11.07: speed dating with eligible virgins, sourced locally and dressed by world acclaimed designer Viktoria Smythe-Griffin in the latest Fall fashions.

Saturday 1am: High speed drag racing in his sports car through the Pegasus subdivision.

Saturday 3am: Hunting.

Saturday daytime: This is unclear, many suspect Prince Forest slept off the excesses of the night in the arms of a man who was dressed as a hare, but this is unsubstantiated.

Saturday 7pm: The Prince attended a special degustation menu at Pompeii with three of the local virgins from speed dating the night before. This time the virgins were dressed in Viktoria Smythe-Griffin haute couture.

Saturday 9pm: Emergence from Pompeii with his antlers out again, visibly drunk and unable to walk without stumbling, wandered towards High Street, partially supported by a particularly pretty blonde virgin.

Saturday 10pm: Attended a screening of the original Superman movie at the Rialto on High Street.

Sunday 1am: Chased trucks down the motorway, bounding on all fours and leaping at the backs of them, tearing their bumper stickers off with his teeth and flinging them into the river.

Sunday 3am: Entered a McDonalds in East Goldfinch and demanded all their chocolate syrup, which of course was handed over instantly, as he is a member of a royal family.

Sunday 4am: howling and cursing at the moon as it arced over the city. This attracted a lot of the city's wildlife and many dogs from the city's backyards, who joined him in a kind of wild howl towards the night sky.

Sunday 6am: walked home, trailed by several squirrels, who seem to have moved into his house.

While many can understand the heartbreak and frustration that Prince Forest is experiencing, there's a general feeling around town that it's time for Prince Forest's curse to be lifted. Of course, in order to do that, the source and cure for the curse would need to be discovered. Is it time for the government to step in? Or is this something the unfortunate Prince Forest needs to do himself? We'll keep you updated, whatever happens.

- Mallory Te Moana reporting

EELMERE SPELLS SUCCESS FOR BRIANNA!

BRIANNA PERSEPHONE WALTERS is being lauded as a local success story after wrestling control of her father's satanic cult from him last Saturday.

The cult, known to the people in the small coastal town of Eelmere simply as the Saturday Sect, had been run by Mr Charles Walters for the last seven decades.

"It was just time for some new blood," Brianna said, in her livestream Q&A session held Sunday to make her new doctrines clear to the sect's followers. "And I don't mean like, virgin blood," she continues, laughing charmingly. "I mean some new ways of thinking. I love my dad, don't get me wrong, but this is 2020, we want to bring this cult from the dark ages and into the solar-powered future. Dad brought a lot of great things to our rituals, but I think we can all agree that his views on werewolves were at best outdated and at worst, downright dangerous. I want to open membership to all of our brethren, whether they be lycanthropic, vampiric, fey or just plain human."

Some of the changes Brianna has brought in includes better recycling stations in the blasted church where the cult meets, a community garden where the cult can spend a couple of shifts a week composting, weeding and producing food for the local soup kitchen. In addition, she wants to open the church up to some more members.

"Recruitment will be key," Brianna said, in a statement written in arcane purple blood on the mirror of this reporter on Monday morning. "We want to show people that what we do isn't just summoning demons, dancing naked around a fire, or baking too many cheesecakes and then eating them all. It's so much more than that. We're the spine of this community and we want to straighten up and hold the community's head high."

The whereabouts of Mr Walters is unclear at this stage, but many of the cult believe he has taken a much-needed vacation at the family's beach house on the island of Write-On-Sea.

Brianna's final statement to This Unusual Life! was in the form of a talking book, which appeared mysteriously on my desk in the magazine's central office. "We know that going forward, the Saturday Sect will be a positive change in the world. Eelmere will be back on the map, you mark my words."

We have faith that this little success story will soon be National news and we offer our sincere congratulations to Brianna as she takes her place on the profane throne.

- Minor Key Marshall reporting

QUESTION CRESSIDA

This Unusual Life! is pleased and elated to continue our engagement with Cressida Flittersocks. Cressida is a noted oracle and witchfinder from the demon realm of Northern Slimetown.

Dear Cressida, it has now been six years since my last truly intimate relations. Is my blood once more usable in potions etc that call for virgins' blood, or will I have to wait for the seventh year to elapse?Anonymous Tapir

Darling Tapir, I'm so glad you got in touch about this. Because as you know, virginity is a state of mind and not at all an all or nothing state of being. If you truly feel you have achieved a second or even third virginity then go ahead and use your own blood.

But the real concern is whether those potions are the correct things to be making now. As the full moon approaches again, and the Dread Starlink once again flies overhead, the time for ritual is now. Use your powers not for potions, but for making a real change in your life. That's right, it's time to defund the police. Your spells can help with the people's movement.

. . .

How many roads must a man walk down?
Sidodli Flange from East Crundle

My dearest Sidoldi,

I know what you're asking appears to be very clear but truly, it depends on the man, your definition of walk, and what constitutes a road. Perhaps give Stephen King's book The Long Walk a quick read? The book you've been reading isn't the right one for you just now.

In the meantime, it's time to reorganise your pantry, darling. Fix up your herbs and spices first and go from there. Remember to thoroughly wipe each shelf as you go and throw out those expired packets of ramen at the back. It may seem like a small thing, but getting the pantry done will give you more of a sense of control in the chaos of your own life as Mercury enters retrograde once more.

Willow Offa-Goode of Midsomer Fallow asks: How can I turn my bedroom into a cosy haven?

Dearest Willow, in order to transform your bedroom from the Hellscape it is now into something more welcoming, first stop storing meat and other foodstuffs in there. Once that is done, banish the kitchen spirits with a quick spray of sage and catnip. Many find a pale or white painted wall to be soothing, so clean the blood and viscera off and try a fresh lick of paint instead.

Now that you have a more comfortable room, I'd like to address the root of your question. Yes, the people you work with have discovered that you are a denizen of the deepest ocean, where the rifts are softly glowing and things from beyond the stars rest and plan their next move, and they're not sure how to talk to you about it. I suggest you host a shared lunch and encourage everyone to bring something from their culture. Then the conversation will naturally allow you to explain why you have brought oysters, raw minnows and nudibranchs.

Question from Sharlene Haunt, Little Shunting.
I inherited my grandmother's secret fruitcake recipe, but I can't get the combination of spices correct. What am I doing wrong? Sharlene

My dearest Sharlene.

You have the combination of spices correct, it's the angle with which you hold the wooden spoon as you stir the batter which is all wrong. It's far too perpendicular, when what you really want is more of a forty five degree angle. Also watch the position of your feet as you add the spices in. Think of the basic ballet positions and move through them intuitively as you bake.

While you're at it, check the feng shui of your kitchen, because I rather think the potted gooseberry is doing more harm than good where you currently have it. Consider repositioning it to a more auspicious spot, and perhaps declutter the fortune zone as well.

Once you've corrected these small issues, your grandmother's secret fruitcake will be a veritable profusion of excellency.

Dearest Cressida,
I pen this question in a moment of most unusual urgency — whence forth may I anticipate an answer?
Yours sincerely
Florian Shuttlebug

Dear Florian,

It is clear to me that your preoccupation with time is based on something far more mundane - when will your Uber arrive is truly the question bothering you. I have read the stars and I see that your

Uber got lost because the numbers on your street are non-Euclidean.

Next time you need a scale and polish, why not just use one of your baby teeth to summon an eldritch dentist? One cannot be too careful with one's teeth after all, and the eldritch sort of dental worker is often the most reliable, and cost-effective as well!

Take care, my dear, and be careful of the bees.

Yours in concern,

Cressida

HOROSCOPES

Jack of Hearts

It's time to dig a new hole. The soft dirt at the back of the garden is an excellent starting place. You'll soon have a perfect, snug and secure burrow for the winter.

Page of Swords

If you keep bringing rainstorms to rain directly on other people's parades, they will form a mob and chase you. One might consider the virtue of a little rain only on the vegetable patches and fruit orchards and letting people have their parades in peace. You can always buy some earplugs, too.

Ace of Spades

The pleasure is to play
No kindness in what they say
From April into May
The best fish is the cray

. . .

Queen of Cups

Making your own pastry is easy with a food processor, just try it. You'll be pleasantly surprised at the results.

The Hierophant

If you're worried about the security of your password, the best option is to use a piece of paper. Write the password on your paper and then set it on fire under the new moon.

The Magician

A white noise machine may help you sleep, but does it help the monsters that live under your bed? Now's a good time to check in with them and ensure that you have a sleep arrangement that works for the four of you.

Missus Bun the Baker

The Summer is acumen in, loudly sing Cuckoo
The vegetable patch is needing rain, softly sing Cuckoo
The ants are in the sugar bowl, roundly sing Cuckoo
The bowls are summer vegetables, just bloody sing Cuckoo

Go Fish

If the goats won't let you sleep, look to Venus. When Venus is ascending you can follow the rays of light to the solution. Don't lose heart now!

JUNE 1956

I SOLD MY BABY ON THE DARK WEB!

A WELL-RESPECTED WESTGHOST father of four has gained attention recently for selling his newest child on the dark web. While local news authorities were quick to condemn the man and the fact that the dark web exists at all, we weren't so sure the story was cut and dry.

This Unusual Life! reached out to Smith Johnson in an exclusive interview to get the real story as concerns little Prunes McGee, who has since been returned to the Johnson household.

"The fact of the matter is," Smith said, somewhat tearfully, "that baby Prunes simply wasn't getting any bigger. We'd been feeding him, taking him to the gym, reading him books about grownups, all the normal things you'd do to encourage a child to grow, but none of it was working. We feared he had one of those 'always a baby' genetic diseases that you heard so much about."

Smith's understudy took over the narration of the story while Smith went to get a drink. "The fact of the matter, as I said," he continued. "Was that our two oldest children had responded well to the normal procedures. So we were out on a limb somewhat, trying to decide what to do."

Smith's wife Beverly had this to add. "Smith's understudy is correct, we just didn't know what to do. I was scouring all the Facebook groups, withholding vaccines, watching celebrity videos on child-rearing, you name it. Then Smith found the answer from an unlikely source."

She pauses to check her lines with the prompt before continuing. "Smith was all over Reddit with his problems, and someone mentioned the dark web to him. At first, we were sceptical but then things started to make a lot of sense."

As a group, Smith, his understudy, Beverly, the line prompt and myself all started an Ask Me Anything converstaion online to recreate the sequence of steps.

"The fact was, our child is special," Smith's understudy told me, as we answered questions around our favourite movies and most coveted roles on the social website. "Unlike many children, little Pruney needs to be traded in order to evolve."

The syndrome Pruney has is largely unknown in official medical circles, bu many online have found overwhelming evidence of its existence. They're calling it Pocket Monster syndrome, after the popular video games and musicals. "Simply put," RightMan2366 said, in a comment on our AMA. "These children need to be traded to grow and change. I've witnessed it many times over the years, and it's always the same. You trade the baby and it grows a few months, you trade it back and your kid's a few years older. They love it, it's really good for them."

Prunes McGee, until a week ago a baby of three months by appearance, but seventeen months old going by the calendar, is now a toddler. The Johnson family admit that it's a little frightening to trade their youngest away on the forum used for all sorts of illegal activities, but none can deny that Prunes is thriving now.

As we close out our AMA and I kiss each member of the family goodbye, the line prompt offers these words to any out there who may be living with Pocket Monster syndrome. "A little more than kin, and less than kind."

Please be in touch if you or anyone you know has this fascinating and largely unknown disorder.

⚘

I MAKE 420 DINNERS IN ONE GO!

IF YOU'VE BEEN ANYWHERE around Pinterest, mommy blogs or keto diet planners, you'll have heard of meal prepping. Meal prepping is the act of mass cooking and producing many packed lunches and dinners so that you don't have to cook throughout the week.

Well, one Westghost local has taken this practice to astounding new heights. "Yes, I commonly make hundreds of meals in one go," Kristoff Marvelo said. "I started meal prepping three months ago, and every time I've started, more and more meals come out of it."

Kristoff is a stay-at-home uncle, living happily with his brood of were-snakes and supporting his partner, who works full time as an anime programmer. "It's the strangest thing," Kristoff continued. "Because I buy the same amount of ingredients each week, chicken to season and bake, lots of broccoli and carrots, courgette if we can source it, and sweet corn. Then I'll start cooking and suddenly I'm boxing up Singapore Fried Noodles, wine soaked radishes and delicately spiced fillets of fish. I have no idea where the food is coming from."

Several neighbours have benefitted from the extra meals as, although Kristoff's brood is ravenous, four hundred meals in a week is still too many. "I've been lucky enough to share the outpourings of my kitchen with some local families who needed it," Kristoff said.

"It's wonderful," Crispino - who lives on Kristoff's street - said when we popped in through his window. "He always meal preps on Sunday afternoon, so we've started a street wide shared dinner thing. We all provide plates of food for Sunday night, and Kristoff distributes the boxed meals. It's kept my family fed for five weeks now, it's just…" he wipes a tear from his eye and sighs. "It's come at a brilliant time, to be honest. We really needed this."

Kristoff recently beat his own record with 420 meals in one day resulting from the same list of ingredients as above. From what we could tell, it just seems to be increasing.

"I'm thinking of filming the whole process, to get to the bottom of it," Kristoff said. "But every time I try to set it up, the camera switches itself off. My partner, well, they said it's not for us to know, but that I should keep on cooking as long as we have need."

This Unusual Life! was lucky enough to sample some of Kristoff's prepared meals and we have to say, the mint sauce and roast lamb was delectable, but his vegan lasagne was the best we've ever had.

🕷

HOROSCOPES

Verisimilitude

When the darkest night closes in around you, know that you are not alone. She's right behind you. We're all right behind you. You're not alone.

Knights

Some mistakes can be erased, some can be covered over with a bit of paper, but some of them require you to burn the city down so that no one ever sees it. I think we all know which kind of mistake you've made.

Six of Pentacles

The box you took from the haunted house needs to be returned. What were you thinking, taking it with you? It's not going to stop whispering.

Marshmallows

When the internet offers you hot chocolate, take it. But stay away from the pop-up advertising cheap coffee. Stay. Away.

Grammarly users

It was honestly the best time. You know, like we all made meals together and sat around this huge table as the sun went down and we were laughing and drinking, and it was so great. I wish you could've been there.

Tiny dancers

Usually, there's a limit to the number of free trials of food delivery services you can get, well. Maybe there isn't for you. You just keep using those vouchers, promo codes and coupons. The universe provides.

Jeff

Jeff, take a day off this week. You won't regret having some Jeff-time.

Albums by Weezer

When you echo the entertainment district of a large Asian city nightlife in your bedroom, you succeed. Embrace the victorious man and go wild on the fresh, hot okonomiyaki, this is what will make your dreams come true.

Green leaves

Someone close to you will ask for a favour this week, it's in your interests to say yes. Your lucky colour is five.

Too many spiders

What if you didn't get a haircut? What if you polished your

glasses less? What if you sold your house and all your belongings and took up academic residency in the forest? The right students will find you.

Cherry pie

It's time for a social media break. The drama will still be there when you come back. You need time to free your mind, find your space and breathe.

Warmest hoodies

As the seasons change, so does your heart, and your body too. It's worth investigating just what kind of thing you can shapeshift into. Now's the time.

QUESTION CRESSIDA

OUR RESIDENT psychic and advice dispenser was lucky enough to renew her contract this month. We are overjoyed that the Capitalism gods have graced us with more time to Question Cressida.

I think my five-year-old child is trying to unionise their classroom, should I stop them?
Lt. Richmond Woodville

My dear Lt, there's very little you can do to prevent five year olds from unionising. It's simply the natural age where humans begin to want to protect their rights as humans and as workers. Instead of stopping them, I would recommend you arm your five year old with some 'workers unite' buttons and let them do as they would.

In regards to your other, unspoken question, the answer is yes. You must in fact, and without delay. If you leave the hole the way it is, all manner of untold nightmares will begin to seep through, and you definitely don't want them staining your new carpet.

. . .

Postage Stamp of Castle-upon-Graveyard has a unique situation, they would like Cressida's help with.

Dear Cressida, My ex is still trying to control me even though I stabbed him to death and he's a ghost now. I've burned his bones and destroyed all remains I can find but he keeps trying to tell me to lose weight and to smile more. Should I do as he says or was I right to murder him?

Yours eternally,

Postage

My darling Postage Stamp,

A brief and effective exorcism performed by thirteen young women will soon see him off. Ensure the women come from all walks of life and that they are young in terms of attitude, not years.

But the larger problem as I see it is that you need to get through that pile of mending that has been stacking up for let's face it, years now. You have plenty of lovely pairs of pants and that nice top you thought you lost is in there. Just set yourself up with some spare buttons, some needle and thread and get to fixing. It won't take nearly as long as you think it will, dear.

OCTOBER 1958

HALLOWEEN IS SPECIAL THIS YEAR

THIS OCTOBER, Halloween is even more special than usual. Thanks to the alignment of both of our moons with the International Space Station and the predicted rise of one of the dread lords of Hell, Dagon. One way or another this Halloween is going to be an extraordinary night.

There are several ways to boost your Halloween preparations this year and we here at This Unusual Life! encourage you to go all out just in case this is our last night on Earth. If we can make it through Zombie Baby Day, we can make it through this, what some experts are calling a Mega-Halloween of Probable Doom.

Firstly, make sure your ghost is the talk of the town by giving them a regular brush down and leaving offerings of small cakes and cold slices of beef each twilight until Halloween.

Secondly, we know you were planning on decorating your house with the usual skeletons, bats and cobwebs, but have you considered floral decoupage? Fresh daffodils, fluffy candy-floss clouds adorned with sweet looking cherubs add a charming atmosphere of love and serenity, which can only be helpful. Soft green bunny rabbits with Christmas presents and snow add an extra touch of pizzazz. There are lots of ideas you can make use of, if any year is the time, it's this one - time to think outside the box and spread some crystal clear antelope cheer.

When it comes to Halloween treats, there's nothing like a bowl of candy mudpies, but break the mould this year by adding some small fish, skewers of fresh fruit or lackadaisical facetious dragons to your bowl. Follow this advice, and your house will be the talk of the Trick or Treaters this year!

Please join our This Unusual Life! Facebook crafting group and share any ideas you have from your family traditions - the best way to survive the upcoming Mega-Halloween of Probable Doom is to be absolutely over the top. There's no such thing as too much!

- Periwinkle Candyfloss

Astrological and Metaphysical Correspondent

SPIDER BREEDERS OF BEACHMONT

Beachmont flatmates Cherry and Ginger have a very interesting story - both of them are world-class spider breeders who used to compete against each other. We sent reporter Flotto Forebough down to Beachmont to get the full story.

"It all started when I was a kid," Cherry says, handing me a cup of tea. "I always liked spiders, and there was one in my bedroom that I taught a couple of tricks. I was seven, and since then I've known it was what I wanted to do with my life. I had a purpose, a calling if you will."

Spider training is an art almost as old as spiders themselves, but of course, it's easier with the larger breeds of spiders rather than the harder to track and control house spiders. Cherry's spider of choice is extra-large Pomeranian tarantulas.

This is what brought her into competition with Ginger, a Battlesea third-generation immigrant from the outer reaches of Stonemoor Heights. Ginger came late to spider breeding. "Yes, I was just out of university and I was taking any job that was going," she says, cutting me a generous slice of Battenburg cake. "I was a pizza delivery person, a flight attendant, worked in a bakery and then this little job in a spider day-care centre. And that was the one where I really found my passion. The spiders were all so sweet and so different. There were some gorgeous Dalmatian spiders, about hip height, and they were my favourites."

They first came head-to-head in the annual Beachmont spider show. "At the time we were both showing Ridgemont funnel webs," Cherry says, plying me with fresh scones with jam and cream. "And she got first in show, and I got second. Then the next year, I'd switched to Corgi daddy long legs, so that I wouldn't be competing against her." They both laugh.

"But I'd switched to the exact same breed!" Ginger giggled. She passed me the bowl of carrot sticks and we all had a good chuckle.

"I was so angry," Cherry said. "But I was lucky enough to win that year, a gorgeous specimen she was, Ser Pepper Beatle von Schram." She indicates a framed photo of a show spider on the wall.

"Well, it went on for a few years," Ginger said. "But then we were both looking for a flat at the same time and happened on this place and were both at the viewing."

"Well, it just made sense to move in together," Cherry said, a wistful look in her eye. They both suggested I try the hummus with flatbread. "The kennels are down the back; we raise spiders together now."

They give me a tour of the flat - it could be any flat in Beachmont, tidy, a little dated and more than anything - homey. It's a cosy place, and it's clear that the two flatmates are very happy cohabitating. A roast meal awaits us as we finish up the tour and we sit down to enjoy it together. Although most of the spiders are kept in a run out the back with the kennels, they have two favourites who live in the house and they're happily cavorting on the rug at dinner. An Irish Setter Wolf spider and a Great Dane Jumper, both of them as tall as myself if they stood on their hind legs.

That's all the article we have from Flotto Forebough, who hasn't been reachable since that night. Enjoy your vacation Flotto!

QUESTION CRESSIDA

FRESH FROM A SOJOURN at her favourite small temple on the edge of the mountains of Direwold, Cressida is back to address your life's concerns.

My mum told me that a flower's stamen is its reproductive organs. I don't want them to get embarrassed, should I make pants for them?
Yours, a small, boring dinosaur

Dear small boring dinosaur,

While it is very sweet of you to be concerned for the flowers, I must assure you that there is simply no need to make pants for the flowers. Flowers are utterly without shame, and therefore don't feel embarrassed at all. The way they lure in those birds and insects, they'll be fine pantsless.

However, I do recommend that you put your efforts into making pants for the small pixies and gnomes that will move into your backyard in a week or so. These two species will need help to establish their new habitats in your yard and clothing will help make them feel welcome and accepted. Also, if you establish early on that you are a friend, they are far less likely to eventually move into your house and oust you. One might also consider putting some saucers of milk out for them and remember to warn any house guests you have about the possibility of fey abductions.

What is the difference between effluent and affluent?
FacQue Https://

My dear Mx Https://.

While considering my answer to this, sweet prince, I have searched long and hard, I have considered my training in anthropology, my study of the dark arts, my deck of tarot cards and the text on the boxes in the cereal aisle of my supermarket. All have led me to two conclusions: effluent has more to do with rivers near farms, affluent more to do with sprawling mansions with ornamental streams.

But the second conclusion is by far the greater. There is a threat not to your life, but to your manner of living. The good news is that if you act quickly and decisively you can prevent interference.

First, paint your front door red and apply the runes of protection that I taught you previously.

Second, move all your belongings to the attic and those that won't fit in there, move onto the roof itself. The ghosts will help you with this if you bribe them with saltwater taffy.

Third, remain in the upper levels of the house until the flood has receded. It will take some time to clean the floors, but the river will leave you many treasures you can make use of in the years to come.

🦟

DECEMBER 1958

(Editor's note, I couldn't see anything dated before this and after June)

DUCHESS OF CHRISTMAS!

PRINCESS LILY, often thought of as the rebellious, party fuelled hellion of the Night Court, showed a new side of herself this week as she invited a host of orphaned children into her palace on the Eastern side of Eastbrigge and warming the hearts of The Nation.

Her Royal Highness, Lily is the second child of Her Venerable Majesty Queen Laurel (may She ever rule these lands) and although many have found her outrageous adventures shocking, this latest debacle is instead one of generosity.

Her Venerable Majesty Queen Laurel (may She ever rule these lands) has not released any official word condemning Princess Lily for her actions, but perhaps the lack of response is in its own way a gentle approval or perhaps reprimand. We here at This Unusual Life! wouldn't dare to venture a theory on what Queen Laurel (may She ever rule these lands) might think.

The orphans were sourced from facilities all over Eastbrigge and, as far as This Unusual Life! can tell, the children were welcomed into the guest wing of the palace, given bedrooms and food, and were invited to a grand Christmas party at the Princess's own cost. The children have been invited to stay permanently with the Princess until suitable adoptive parents have been located.

There is no evidence that any of the children have been eaten at all, and it seems the Princess is deviating from her family's expectations and heritage once again by being utterly sincere and generous.

Naturally, this kind of behaviour is not what we have come to expect from the Royal Family, but the nation has warmed to the Princess in the wake of this unexpected and frankly extraordinary act of kindness. This Christmas, we urge you to take inspiration from our magnanimous Princess and do what you can to help those in need around you.

We suggest donating to your local mission for the poor, Society for Prevention of Cruelty to Animals, rape crisis, women's refuge or werewolf rehoming programme.

- Cedric Ramekin reporting

HERO MUM SHOT WITH A CROSSBOW TO SAVE THE WORLD

WHEN KAYLEE ELIZABETH JIAN, the Light Bringer, came into her full power a few years ago, she rocked the world. It was impossible to ignore her impressive battles against vampires, ghouls, demons and all nature of evil.

However, two weeks ago a dark prophecy came to the attention of the Light Bringer, which seemed to spell the end of the world altogether. Many assumed that Kaylee herself would be the one to resolve the mess of the prophecy, as she had several previous calamities and threatened catastrophes.

Kaylee is known around town as an inveterate supporter of the amateur arts. As well as being the Chosen One, Kaylee is often to be seen at the local school's productions and producing delicious cupcakes for the local bake sales - when she isn't busy battling the forces of evil.

Together with her ragtag team of loveable misfits, she patrols the night. In case you're not familiar, her team includes: Amir, the bumbling but kind-hearted witch, Annie-May, the hacker and all-round tech whizz, always thinking outside the box, who many say was proud to work alongside her mother. And finally, Bobby, everyone's favourite, who, as well as being a strong fighter and charismatic vlogger, is also in possession of a mysterious magical tattoo.

Over time it became clear that the prophecy had a loophole. Kill the Bringer of Light, mother of two, and stop the sky falling. Many have theorised that had the sky fallen, the stars themselves enflamed and the moon cracked in half, that it truly would have been the end of life on Earth, but like, for real this time.

"It's horribly sad," Bobby said, in one of the last episodes uploaded to his popular web series. "We really tried everything we could think of to find another way out, but there was nothing we could do. I really miss her, you know? I've been baking almost every day in her memory."

Finally, it was Kaylee's teenage daughter, Annie-May, that took up the fated crossbow.

"She was screaming and crying," witness Moffat Patrick said, in an anonymous call to This Unusual Life! "She kept saying 'this is the only way' and Kaylee was so shocked she didn't say anything, just stood there, crying a single tear, her lip glossed mouth pouting slightly, finally she made the slightest inclination of her head. Then Annie-May let the bolt loose and Kaylee was down."

Annie-May was unavailable to comment, but she has been active on social media in the wake of the event, replying to other Chosen Ones who have come forward with words of praise and condolences for her widow and two children, using the hashtag #LightBringer.

"Thanks for all your work, Kaylee, I'll never forget the time we fought Krampus. Forever in my heart" tweeted Holly McMaster, Swordswoman of the Modern Age.

We certainly lost a hero that night, but here at This Unusual Life! we humbly thank Kaylee for her sacrifice. One last time saving the life of the entire planet. To be a Chosen One is a difficult calling at the best of times, but when it comes with a life-ending prophecy, we can only imagine the heartache.

Our thoughts and prayers with Annie-May and the other misfits commonly seen helping and comedically bantering with Kaylee. We are sorry for your loss. If you'd like to donate to Annie-May's charity and help others affected by the tumultuous lives of Chosen Ones, set a picture of a polar bear in your front window.

7 THINGS FROM THE 80S SURE TO MAKE YOU FEEL NOSTALGIC

1. The ambient smell of Christmas stockings first thing in the morning - what happened to that smell? Every time I sniff a Christmas stocking, I'm reminded of the eighties.
2. Snap bracelets - They were always being banned!
3. iPhones - who among us can't remember being given a new iPhone in 1987? Those things were the number one must-have toy of the holidays. There were even riots in toy shops!
4. Stickers! From fuzzy ones, to the ones you scratched and they'd smell like bananas, to the ones that projected a rainbow of Italian-made pony holograms onto the ceiling. Everyone had a sticker collection.
5. Mix tapes - how many hours did you spend recording music off the radio, patching together pieces of wildflowers and grass, binding it with the tears of your youthful pain and carefully hand printing the cassette liner to give to that special someone?
6. Rotary telephones - I had one in the shape of a pair of human lips. When you lifted the receiver you saw the teeth and the tongue, soft and damp. I spent so many hours on that thing, gossiping with friends!

7. Pen pals - many lament that the art of letter writing is lost, but the eighties were a boom time for pen pals. Industrious letter writers loved trading stickers, tales of weird goblins and small birds who could sing all sorts of songs, spirits summoned, wills diminished. The magic of communication was the essence of the eighties.

BYTOWN PORTRAIT ATTACKS

A special This Unusual Life! report follow up

WE PREVIOUSLY REPORTED the bizarre and senseless attacks on family portraiture.

This Unusual Life! is pleased to be able to report we have a follow-up. Our previous investigations revealed a link between each family who have had a portrait defaced, the Bytown City Mall portrait service.

Although it is shocking to relay this update to you, we feel that it is of the utmost importance that we do. Our foremost portraiture reporter, Tiger Smith, went undercover in the portrait service in the interest of finding the truth of this story.

In their time working for the photographer, situated in the depths of the Bytown City Mall, Tiger discovered something unexpected. In addition to a disturbingly large cache of frosted donuts in the photo printing machinery, Tiger discovered the insides of the photography equipment used for capturing photos to be eldritch in creation.

"It's like the camera is just a plastic shell and inside there are these weird clumps of mud and twigs, string twisted into knots and polished stones," Tiger reported from a secure location. "It looked more like my Uncle Abigail's house parties at Midwinter. You know, she's a witch and all, so there's a lot of magic work in the garden and tying knots to bind things. I hadn't expected that inside the cameras, especially since they somehow still take fantastic photos."

When This Unusual Life! called the portrait service anonymously for comment, they had this to say. "We've never said we're not witches who are using the eyes of the people in the photographs to drain the emotions of the household to fuel our dark purposes. Simply put, the fact remains that we deliver a quality product. Our portraits always have everyone looking the same way, everyone smiling and there's never one of those awkward shots where one person's eyes are closed. In the end, isn't that what really matters?"

Soon after this conversation, Tiger Smith arranged for the This Unusual Life! team to have a group portrait taken together. It really is a stunning photo, and we've not particularly noticed a decrease in the amount of emotions we feel. Tiger Smith has since resigned their position at the magazine and opened a new franchise in Ye Olde Bytown Malle, taking family portraits.

- Valpy Bennet reporting

JANUARY 1959

HOROSCOPES FOR THE YEAR 2020

SHEEP PEOPLE

The mouse needs new batteries, just go and pick up some new ones and replace them. The mouse will work way better, and things will become clearer.

Minotaurs

It's never too early to start celebrating your birthday. Start now, and incite everyone to birthday party with you. Ice cream, candy, cake and unicorns. All can be yours! Seize the birthday!

Doppelgangers

It takes a whole day, but the rewards are worth it
It takes a whole day, but you have what you need
If it takes a whole day, you're sure to have seen them
Use your whole day, make it be what you need

Crabs of the deep

Three cups of sugar

Half a cup of milk, bring to a boil

Add in 115g of butter, a half cup of condensed milk and a couple of pinches of salt

Boil low until the mixture reaches 120 degrees, let it cool to 90 or so then mix with an electric mixer, pour into a greased pan and cut up when set

Beast Kings

Time to organise that high tea, invite your friends and have that talk. It's time. Trust us. They'll bring really good cakes. They'll understand.

Too precious for this world

There's no people like show people, like no people I know
Everything about me is appealing
Everything you've heard is just hearsay
I've got a blank space, baby…

Best sign

Some years are for striving, some are for thriving and some are for lizards. I think we all know what 2020 is going to be for you.

Make war not love

You're so cute, how cute are you? No, listen, don't argue, you're adorable. Just own it.

Goat people

2020 will be the year you can transform into your final form. Make sure you know which form you'd like to take and make the proper preparations. Do you need a fire stone? A thunder stone? Do you need to go to the forest and stand near a special rock? Just make sure you're prepped.

. . .

Vase of flowers

Karaoke machine, bucket hat, fishnet stockings, a piece of cake, wine glass, tote bag, elder god, and so on.

She's a little fish

You need to pick a new song for your recital. It turns out one of the organisers got confused and assigned your song to a few people, so you want to pick something new that will let you stand out. It's okay, you got this. You know which song will work.

LARKSPUR AND HOLLY'S COSY BREAKFAST

EARLY THIS MORNING social media was abuzz with photos and rumours as Prince Larkspur made a public appearance with Holly Albert, a half fey, half human student of Rocksbridge university. The two shared a cosy breakfast at Sunshine Poppy Café, a modest eatery downtown.

The two sported dark sunglasses and wide smiles, seeming very comfortable with each other as they ate. Sources who were on site report that Larkspur ordered a seafood platter and Holly ordered a soft-boiled egg with toast soldiers. Larkspur playfully fed her a shrimp, a moment captured in this sweet photo.

(Editor's note: the photo paperclipped to this article appears to be of an old man with a thick beard holding up a sizable trout and smiling at the camera. Behind him there is a vast lake and distant mountains.)

Holly is reported to have touched Larkspur on the arm and shoulder multiple times over the hour they spent eating and chatting, and the two certainly seem to be snuggled up together. The happy couple were whisked away by a private car and it seems that he took her back to the modest Summer palace where he spends much of his time.

We're happy that the prince and the student seem to be happy, and it looks relatively certain that he won't carve her heart out with his knife, for now at least!

- Cedric Ramekin reporting

WE THOUGHT MY SON WAS IN A COMA, WE WERE WRONG!

It's NOT every day you get a miraculous resolution to a traumatic medical condition. But that's exactly what happened for this East Goldmarsh family.

The Finches, a seemingly ordinary polyamorous family of five, at first thought their son Robert's constant falling down was epilepsy, then they got a diagnosis of narcolepsy. In an exclusive interview with the entire family, This Unusual Life! got the full story.

Meet Robert, a normal twelve-year-old kid with lots of love for life. A member of the school's baseball team, dance club and cryptid categorisation club and a well-liked classmate.

"As he grew up, he didn't seem worried about his affliction," Bryce, father of Robert says. "He was a happy kid, really gregarious, you know? He was always making friends with the neighbours, all the kids in his class. He was normal, you know, except for the narcolepsy."

But last year, something extraordinary happened. "We thought he'd gone into a coma," Yuki, Robert's father said. "Well, actually we thought it was narcolepsy, but then he didn't wake up. After a few days, we had him moved into a hospital."

The future looked grim for Robert, now thirteen, as doctors

couldn't find the reason for the coma, or any indication that he would snap out of it.

"We started planning a funeral," Midge, little sister of Robert added. "I wanted to bury him in the back garden."

"Yes, but then he visited you, didn't he, Midgey?" Robert prompts. The little girl, just five years old, nodded.

"In my bedroom. I just woke up in the morning and he was there, at the end of my bed. He told me not to worry."

"He visited us next," Valerie, Robert's mother, says. "Just appeared, all ghostly like and insubstantial. I thought he'd died. But he said don't worry, mum, I'm still alive."

"That's when we knew he was something really special," Bryce said.

Robert was an astral projector. His spirit has the ability to leave his body and travel in the aether, or spirit world. "In fact, he'd probably been doing it his whole life," Yuki said. "We just didn't understand, or he wasn't able to fully form in front of us."

"It actually explained how he knew some of our neighbours quite so well," Valerie added. "He seemed to know things I wasn't sure they would have mentioned to a small child."

Astral projection is still a relatively new evolution for humans, and the Finches were eager to share their story with us to further knowledge and understanding. Some speculate that astral projection connects a human's spirit more closely to Death and the afterlife, but much is still unproven.

"There's really nothing to be worried about," Bryce insists. "He can control where and when he goes, and he's a polite kid. He wouldn't intrude on private things."

Robert is one of a growing number of children hitting puberty and discovering strange powers. This Unusual Life! is planning a series spotlighting the successes and struggles of these special teens. We encourage our readers to come forward and share their stories if they have a family member or friend going through something similar.

Please refer to form Q in the addendum if you'd like to share the story of a tween developing strange powers.

- Mallory Te Moana reporting

※

FEBRUARY 1960

5 CUTE STORIES FROM VALENTINE'S DAY

1. Royal watchers confirm that Prince Larkspur has not yet eaten the heart of his mortal girlfriend Holly Albert. Instead, the handsome and utterly charming prince took his lady love to a private screening of the new Apple Pie Recipe at the Odeon downtown. So romantic!

2. Bob and Sally have been married for 32 years, but the romance is still alive! They celebrated this Valentine's Day by setting out seed for wild birds in the community bird feeders and trimming the berm on their street. Way to keep the magic going, Sally and Bob!

3. Under the cobbles of Main Street, the under dwellers celebrate Valentine's as they always do, with a stirring dance and roasted rat meat. You can roast your own rat at home to honour their traditions.

4. The department store of Vaughan and Splendid opened their hands and hearts to the general public this year. Staff were seen handing out sugar cookies decorated with red and green frosting and festive images of spiders. Those who accepted the generous gift have reported songs haunting their dreams and a pleasant peppermint scent in the morning when they wake up.

5. Andy, Carrie, Milo, Alexandra and Olivia celebrated their devotion to each other with a moonlit walk on the beach, followed by a picnic of fresh fruit, cauliflower grilled cheese and hand-picked blueberries. The devoted family finished the night with an ancient ritual to the Old Ones, ensuring a blessing for their shared relationship.

HIGH FLYING TWEEN

Stonepine locals were recently bewildered by the sight of a small child flying through the air above the streets on a recent mid-afternoon. Several Stonepine sources saw fit to signal to our staff to spread news of this strange situation.

On investigation, the child was discovered to be Shravan Xhosa, local tween and enthusiast of the history of the Trans-Atlantic. We caught up with Shravan and his family on a balmy Tuesday midnight in their comfortable Stonepine home.

"We discovered he could fly at the family Kwanzaa celebration," Shravan's father Jabari said. The family home is a palatial double-storey mansion on the well-kept and elegant Douglas Avenue. "Obviously it was a shock to start with, but once we realised he knew how to land safely we started to allow him to experiment outside.

Shravan's Aunty Nuru elaborated. "We don't know how this started, in fact we're sure he's known how to do this for a long time. But he was hiding it."

Shravan himself is a non-verbal child with autism and thus hasn't been able to tell his family any details himself, but the family are quick to assure our reporters that he absolutely loves to fly.

"He's retrieved frisbees and tennis balls from the roof of the house," Jabari said. "From all the houses on the street really, the local kids were overjoyed."

"And one day he brought me a protea flower from the very top of our tree," Nuru added. "It was exceptionally beautiful. I can never reach the ones from right up the top of the tree."

When asked if there were any concerns about Shravan's safety Nuru shook her head. "He knows to avoid powerlines and not to go too high. We've shown him photos of helicopters and airplanes and made it clear he should avoid them."

But it's not all flowers and tennis balls. The Xhosa family tells of a particular problem that most children wouldn't experience.

"Drones are just the worst," Jabari said. "They buzz around and Shravan can't stand the sound of them. We have asked the neighbours not to operate them, but the park at the end of the road is very popular with hobbyists."

He shakes his head and sighs, reaching to adjust a stray curl on his gorgeous head of hair. "We're going to write to the council and ask if they can put up a sign."

Our visit finished with a display of Shravan flying over the front lawn and the roof of the house. Our reporters agree that Shravan was a figure of joy, turning loops and barrel rolls and laughing with pure enjoyment. To see it was to understand some of that joy, and this reporter is confident that whatever the future holds for little Shravan, it's going to be amazing.

(*Editor's note: there was a photo stapled to this article which showed three cats sitting on the back of a piano.*)

Shravan is one of a growing number of children hitting puberty and discovering strange powers. This Unusual Life! is planning a series highlighting the successes and struggles of these special teens. We encourage our readers to come forward and share their stories if they have a family member or friend going through something similar.

Please refer to form Q in the addendum if you'd like to share the story of a tween developing strange powers.

- Mallory Te Moana reporting

MY POLTERGEIST IS MY FRIEND

MOST HAUNTED HOUSES are a cause for fear, sleepless nights and other inconveniences. But a haunted house isn't a problem for area man Balin Southerfield, 36, of Vertloch.

When I entered the tidy, modern townhouse, I immediately felt a chill over the back of my neck. To my eye it's a totally normal, KonMari'd house with good natural light and here and there some mementoes from Balin's trips overseas.

Balin, a software architect who is currently wishing he hadn't agreed to this interview, leads me into a cosy study with a view over the river. The house is furnished in Germanic Science Fiction style, and Balin mentions that it's been featured in several fan magazines. I take a seat on a lightly plush couch shaped like a meteor and Balin starts talking.

"I first knew the house had an entity in it, other than me, a week after I moved in. I was upstairs in the bedroom, and I live alone. You should know that before I continue." I nodded, knowing that, and he continued. "I was mostly asleep, like, five minutes into sleep and I heard this banging noise from downstairs. Well, I didn't think too much of it, but then there was a creaking on the stair, and the door to my bedroom flapped open and shut a few times. I knew then it was something supernatural because my door is a sliding one, modelled after the original Star Trek series. You know, if it had been a German production."

"So this noise?" I prompted, gently.

"Oh sure, well I sat up in bed and I said, 'hey you, what're you doing here?' and the thing like, whooshed through the room, like it was a huge wind inside the house. It made all my hair stand on end, and I'm very ticklish, so I started giggling. That's when I saw her."

Balin pauses, smiling, his eyes twinkle with recollection. "She stood in the corner, near the replica German spaceship I use as a wardrobe. She'd never had anyone giggle like that when she revealed herself before, so she was laughing too. She came and sat on the bed and we just giggled like five-year-olds, you know?"

Since that night, a year and a half ago, Balin and Lena have been living harmoniously together. "She's great, she reminds me if I'm heading out and I've forgotten a jacket or my keys. She keeps me company while I cook and she has the most beautiful singing voice. Since she's bound to the house, I take lots of photos while I'm out and upload them to the smart TV so she can look at where I've been and kind of experience it herself."

He shows me some photos of the two of them together, but due to the difficulty of spectral photography, Lena largely comes out as a glowing orb next to Balin's face.

"I just want people to be more open minded about the spirits in their houses," Balin said. "Sure, some of them are actively trying to possess your trees and steal your children into an unseeable, unknowable shadow realm, but I genuinely think it's because they're misunderstood. Maybe if more people took the time to laugh a little with their poltergeists they'd discover that we can all just get along."

As he escorts me out of the house, I get a goodbye of sorts from Lena. Typically shy with strangers, Balin is extravagantly pleased that Lena has made an effort to make herself known to me. As I pick up my cravat and poncho from the coat rack, a beret is flung to the floor near me. I look around and see the shadow of a woman, hovering in a corner of the ceiling. I give her a smile and wave and she wiggles her fingers at me, shyly.

It certainly doesn't seem that this poltergeist is any danger at all. I believe Balin is right, and that with a little understanding, a little humour and a little patience, we could all make peace with our troubled spirits.

- Rami Centaur reporting

ADVERTORIAL

Zombie Trousers!

NEVER WORRY ABOUT whether or not you should wash your denim again with the pants that do it for you!

Many so-called fashionistas have said that true denim should never be washed. We say 'that sounds icky, what if you drop food?'

Embrace the icky and remove it with new, patented Zombie Trousers! They'll get up in the night and walk to the washing machine when they're ready for a clean. Never worry again, about anything at all.

QUESTION CRESSIDA

As EVER, This Unusual Life! is gloriously excited to bring you Question Cressida. Cressida Flittersocks is a noted oracle and witch fancier from the hallowed realm of Northern Slimetown.

Dear Cressida,

I've met the perfect boy, but he's totally going out with the head cheerleader. I know she's wrong for him. She even wears short shorts!

Should I be mixing a love portion, to catch him.

A truth potion, to show him how horrible his girlfriend is to everyone.

Or a Polymorph potion so I can take her place?

Lovestruck-Alchemist

Dear Lovestruck-Alchemist,

You actually have two incredibly important paths ahead of you. The question isn't between the options you offered in your missive, but a deeper one. Do you wish to use your gifts in alchemy for the greater good, or only for self-advancement?

Please take some time and really examine this conundrum, for it will guide you through your future. If you decide that self-advancement is the true path for you, then you must use a truth potion to expose his girlfriend and then immediately follow up with a love potion in order to ensnare him to your will.

However, if you decide that your gifts and potions would be best used for the betterment of humankind, you mustn't interfere with someone else's relationship. Although you say you know she's wrong for him, we can never truly understand what is going on between two other people. Perhaps in the fullness of time, you will see that this boy isn't truly perfect, or you will see that you deserve more than a boy who can't see past your gruff and slightly unkempt exterior, and find someone more appropriate. Remember that although high school feels like the most important thing in the world right now, there is more to life, and in a few years you may not even remember this boy's name.

Whatever path you choose, know that I love and support you. Take your time with this one, dear, it's a complicated conundrum.

Advice please:
Last weekend some mates and I had a bet about who could hook the biggest fish. I was out fishing around 47°9'S, 126°43'W, and hooked some great sea beast of unfathomable size, tall enough to block the sun and shroud the sea in the darkness of wings that stretched from horizon to horizon. I went to take a photo, but my camera melted into burning plastic when focused on my catch.
How to convince my mates I did catch the biggest fish on our lads' weekend without them dismissing it?
- The one that got away.

Dear one that got away,
Oh, how familiar I am with this agony! Of course, it would be wonderful to have a photograph of this magnificent "fish" but

SOME THINGS ARE NOT MEANT TO BE RECORDED. In terms of recording your achievement, I might suggest you try and capture a description of it in words, but do not attempt to sketch it.

I know your ego demands recognition from your "lads", and for that I have but one piece of advice. Look within yourself as deeply as you can. This might take several attempts, for self-reflection is exceptionally difficult. If you can look deeply into your motivation for wanting this recognition you might find that you are lacking something deeper. When was the last time you felt happy in your skin? When was the last time you really let yourself feel what you needed to feel? Be kind to yourself and acknowledge your needs. You might have a surprising outcome.

Stay in touch, my dear and let me know if the nightmares get more real.

MARCH 1960

VENERABLE QUEEN LAUREL (MAY SHE EVER RULE OUR LANDS) STEPS OUT IN STYLE

HEADS TURNED and fashion designers went back to their drawing boards last Tuesday when Venerable Queen Laurel (may She ever rule our lands) made a fantastic public appearance in a startlingly wonderful new gown.

Bees!

That's right, bees.

The gorgeous bee dress had a sweetheart neckline, off the shoulder full sleeves, a sweeping skirt with a high slit and seemed to be made entirely of bees. One assumes that Venerable Queen Laurel (may She ever rule our lands) used her near-infinite magical powers to ensure the bees stay in place, although every now and then a bee or two would flitter off her body and then return, creating a charming shimmer effect.

This Unusual Life! has learned the dress was designed by the Venerable Queen Laurel (may She ever rule our lands) herself.

This gown has instantly started a new fashion craze, with many fashion-forward thinking people trying to emulate the look with garden bees. Unfortunately, as many would-be DIYers were quick to discover, bees are hard to train to stay in place on a human body.

We're sure this look will spur many lookalikes and imitators, but we're sure you'll agree, as you look at our exclusive photos, that no one can pull off this look as well as our wonderful and Venerable Queen Laurel (may She ever rule our lands).

- Cedric Ramekin reporting

(Editor's note: the photos clipped to this article are a series of pictures demonstrating how to reupholster the seat cushion of a mahogany dining chair.)

🕷

HOROSCOPES

RAT

Your leeks are almost ready to harvest. Just make sure you keep an eye on the ghosts - they might come in the night and help themselves to your leeks.

Ox

More dangerous than you appear, this month people will try to test you. Try to remember not to gore them outright.

Tiger

That old manuscript of yours? The one with the zombie retellings of fairy tales? It's time to dust it off, give it an edit and shop it around. Zombie fairies are really big right now in the publishing circles.

Rabbit

You are the true Chosen One. Await the signal, then take up your weapon and bring justice to this world.

Dragon

Hey Dragon, you're looking really good this week. I made a playlist for you on Spotify, you just need to sign in and you should have a notification with the link to it. I uh, it has some stuff on there I want to say to you, but nothing can express it as well as these songs can. Sorry, this is so awkward!

Snake

The swell of the waves on the shore of the city will bring treasures just for you. Ensure you're there at sunrise and sunset as often as you can manage until the next full moon. There are things you need.

Horse

Vigour, comic book, teddy bear, caravan, Pokemon, rubber ducks, pleasures of the flesh, landline, jacket, blanket, lightbulb

Sheep

If you place a fragment of a stone from the street you lived on when you were ten years old under your pillow you can free yourself from the recurring dream. It's up to you to set that monster back to rest.

Monkey

That's never going to heal if you don't stop picking it!

Rooster

Keep your fluids up, early to bed, take painkillers when you need them and get plenty of rest.

. . .

Dog

Just as the daffodil slumbers through the Winter under the ground, so can you bury yourself deep under the grass and hibernate if you choose to. Just be sure and let your loved ones and workplace know before you do it.

Pig

The following must be read aloud for full efficacy:
Banana demon, please appease the full horror of the night
Banana demon, do not linger after you have helped
Banana demon, please accept the offering I have made

- Leave out a bunch of free-range bananas before you go to bed.

PRINCE LARKSPUR SPOTTED HANGING ABOUT IN JEWELLERY STORES

Could wedding bells be in the future for Prince Larkspur and his lucky lady, Holly? Several people witnessed the charismatic and heroic prince lurking in the shadows at the Capital's number one jewellery store last Wednesday.

Bunchkin, who works at Master Champagne's Home for Gems tweeted this: "OMG you wouldn't believe it, but Larkspur practically grabbed my arm as I walked back from lunch today. He wanted to look at rings. Squee!"

Bunchkin's manager, Chardonnay LaCroissant, reached out to This Unusual Life! at a nearby train station.

"He spent at least two hours loitering in the shadows before he reached out," she said. "Anyone could tell he had the jitters. Of course we were only too happy to stay open as late as he needed to, and after three hours scanning through our assortment of sparkly rings, he chose a very fine selection."

Of course, we pressed Chardonnay for details of the ring but her lips were sealed with professional discretion. And possibly a magical silence command from the handsome young prince!

"All I can tell you is whoever is the recipient of that ring is going to be a very happy person indeed," were the words of wisdom Chardonnay left us with.

The staff here at This Unusual Life! are very hopeful that there will be a joyous announcement from the royal family quite soon.

- Cedric Ramekin reporting

HAS ZOMBIE BABY DAY LOST ITS TRUE MEANING?

• opinion

THIS WEEK, as I'm sure you'll have noticed, our stores and super-markets once again became flooded with Zombie Baby Day merchandise a good five weeks before Zombie Baby Day itself. Now, I love Zombie Baby Day as much as the next doomed soul, but I can't be alone in wishing we could contain the celebrations to just the day itself, can I?

As a child, I always looked forward to Zombie Baby Day - not just as a day off school, or a day when my entire family could huddle together in the attic of our locked down and barricaded house, but as a time of great joy. Because what greater happiness can there be in this world, than the knowledge that Zombie Babies don't just disappear into nothingness, but they live year round in the sea, and one day a year they crawl out onto land and look for people to chew on?

Call me a nostalgic old softie, but it just warms my heart. It makes you think of the really important things in life, such as what happens when we die, why we should never go into the ocean and of course, the importance of wearing sturdy, knee high leather boots.

But when I go into the local department store and see the collec-tions of zombie plushies, the cutesy pennants that read 'don't visit here, Zombie Babies!' and the novelty chocolates, I just get annoyed. It's all mass consumerism now, companies just trying to squeeze as many pennies out of us as they can. And that sucks! I even saw 'Hope you don't die!' Zombie Baby Day greeting cards yesterday. That's ridiculous. Your loved ones should know you don't want them to die eaten by a zombie baby without a chintzy card.

I'm calling for all the readers of This Unusual Life! to take a stand. Let's not let the greeting card companies turn this important day into another reason to buy and exchange chocolates. Let's keep Zombie Baby Day the way it's supposed to be - huddled in the attic of a heavily fortified house with our nearest and dearest, hoping to be spared another year.

I think we'd all be much better for it.

- Rami Centaur

PRINCE FOREST IN TEARY TELL ALL

The Cursed Prince, some call him. Others call him the Tragic Beauty, some call him a star cursed fool of love, but to us, he'll always be Prince Forest, because that's his name.

We recently received this article by messenger aardvark, and after verifying the sources were real, we have decided to print it in its entirety. Please note this is a This Unusual Life! Exclusive, and we don't commonly accept submissions by aardvark. We're sure you'll agree, on reading, that this is a special case.

I caught up with Prince Forest last Sunday night when he appeared in my dining room unannounced. I hadn't known he was going to be visiting, and in fact, never let him into the house. But these things aren't important when it's about royalty after all. I'm not even a journalist, but he asked me to listen to him, and if I liked, to write it down and share it somehow.

"I just feel so lonely," he said. He's a breathtaking creature up close. His eyes pools of star-touched brown, as if you were gazing at the most beautiful tree in the world under the night sky. His mouth has a sensual voluptuousness that I couldn't help but stare at, and of course, in that glossy thatch of chestnut curls, the gorgeous nubs of his antlers.

"It's just this curse, you know?" he continued. "I literally can't be close to anyone for any length of time, and it's really tiresome. When I was younger, like, say a thousand years ago, it didn't bother me that much, because I was only after thrills anyway. But now I just feel empty."

I offered him a raspberry bark tea and he sighed into it dramatically but undeniably alluringly. "The thing is," he said. "I actually thought that Prince Larkspur might be the one, and I know it's stupid to say that now. But on some level he really *got* me, you know? Have you ever had that?"

I commented that I did understand, and I have had that. For ten minutes he stared into my eyes and I was unable to move or speak aside from the gentle movement I needed to continue breathing. Finally, he looked away.

"Yeah, so you know what it feels like, and now we've split apart, and he has a new girlfriend and I just feel like this is it for me. I'll actually never find love, and there's nothing I can do about it."

My heart went out to Prince Forest then - not literally, thankfully, he didn't seem in the mood for casual slaughter - but metaphorically. I offered him a packet of chocolate biscuits, which he ate, wrapper and all, in one mournful swallow.

"I don't know how to break the curse," he said, finally. Maybe three hours later. "I've tried a lot of things, and none have worked. I don't suppose you have any ideas?"

I suggested that maybe people could write in and suggest curse breakers, and he shrugged one shoulder and sighed. "I mean, what's the worst that could happen?" he said. "May as well give it a try. Tell whoever you want about this, spread it wide. I don't give a shit any more."

Then, abruptly, he stood up from the table and put me to sleep with a spell. I woke up a day later - my house was absolutely spotless and the pantry was full of luxurious and delicious foods.

So, I've sent this article through to you to publish, and maybe you'd consider running a competition or something where people could suggest curse breaking rituals? Our beloved Prince Forest needs our help.

Please do get in touch with This Unusual Life! *if you have any rituals, spells, charms or other suggestions for ways for Prince Forest to dispel his heartbreaking curse. We'll offer a cash prize. More details on page 887*

(Editor's note: I couldn't find page 887 in the shoebox)

TEN GREAT TIPS TO ENHANCE YOUR HABITAT SLIGHTLY

0. Use removable wall hooks to store more of your things vertically. Consider this method for your reusable canvas bags, your caterpillars or cursed wooden masks

1. Salt circles aren't just for when you're actively threatened by demons. A circle of salt around your house can lend an air of sophistication as well as protection for your house. Try using Himalayan rock salt for an extra hip touch
2. Bleeding walls can really stain the carpets, consider putting in linoleum or easy clean tiles to prevent dangerously slippery floors and unsightly stains
3. Carefully and mindfully folding your clothes can awaken them to your emotions. Make sure you fold with love, not anger, or next time you put that shirt on, or it might make you commit homicide!
4. Want your house to smell amazing, all the time? Try an essential oil burner - these little contraptions are about the size of a breadbasket, and only require an hour of chanting each day to activate
5. Attract birds and other desirable wildlife to your garden

with elevated bird feeders. Remember, the higher you place the food, the bigger the birds - you'll want at least a fifty-foot pole to get the most beautiful whale birds

6. Sick of scrubbing for hours? A quick incantation on your scrubbing brush will banish unsightly mould in moments. Simply chant: 'oh dread Master, who lies dreaming in the dead city, allow this brush to be your hand'. Works every time!

7. Saggy couch cushions can make your living area look sad and dated. This is easily fixed, just stuff the cushions with debris and leaves you've raked from your yard. This solves two problems at once and takes very little time.

8. Not using your spare room? Maybe it's the unquiet spirits thirsting for vengeance stopping you. Ask around locally to find the best local high priest for a ritual banishment- or if you're low on goats, try the Make-A-Wish Foundation.

9. Place an upside-down wall hook on the outside of your shower to keep the shower liner in place.

STORM OF THE CENTURY

THE METEOROLOGICAL SOCIETY has issued several warnings to the Southern part of The Nation. Residents of Northburn, Aldspring and Stonemoor, in particular, are likely to be hit by the now infamous Doll Cyclone which has been battering the coasts of Lochmist for three months.

Reports from the coast have been sporadic, with locals largely fleeing the area after the storm broke. The Cyclone at first appeared to be a normal storm, with darkened clouds and high winds. However, once the clouds broke the residents realised the clouds held haunted dolls.

The dolls fell to Earth at first quite slowly, with passing drizzles of small plastic collectable dolls popular with pre-tweens. Once the storm set in, the rain increased to 11.5-inch fashion dolls, rag dolls and finally, at the height of the storm, clown dolls.

Although many residents at first welcomed the dolls into their homes, it soon became clear that the dolls themselves were possessed by strange and dangerous spirits. Many reported, via social media, that the dolls were picking up knives and threatening the family, standing at the foot of the bed while people slept, or running about quickly in the periphery of people's visions on unknown errands. The plague of dolls has slowly moved inland from the coasts of

Lochmist. The training of exorcists has been fast-tracked by the government to counteract the infestation.

As we know from the situation in Lochmist, the best way to resist the dolls is to destroy any dolls that fall from the sky. Whether they are less than an inch tall or the size of your youngest child, show no mercy to the rain dolls.

The Meteorological Society also suggests practising some basic wards and exclusion spells if you have the talent for it. Please remember to look out for the more vulnerable members of your community during the oncoming storm. The elderly are particularly disposed to adopting cute dolls into their houses, and they may not understand the danger.

QUIZ!

Which member of a 90s Boy Band is your Illuminati secret master?

WHAT'S your ideal first date?
A: Dinner and a movie
B: Blood ritual and rampage
C: Attending a show or musical
D: Digging your toes into the soil

Your favourite holiday destination would be...
A: A tropical island
B: A haunted castle in the East of Europe
C: A big city in a country I've never visited before
D: Deepest forest

If your house could be anything in the world, it would be...
A: A mansion with a private movie theatre and a fully stocked wine cellar
B: A penthouse apartment with cutting edge tech
C: A very small cave, several miles from the nearest human civilisation

D: Surrounded by trees

Pick a 90s sitcom character
A: Joey from Friends
B: Dracula from That's so Dracula!
C: The sister from Mr Mike's Medicine Mayhem
D: Uncle Phil from Fresh Prince of Bel Air
E: The staircase from Full House

Mostly A
Congrats! Taylor Hanson is your secret Illuminati Master! He's a down home boy with great looks, amazing hair, and a strong family centred heart. You can't go wrong with this one.

Mostly B
Wow! Your secret Illuminati Master is none other than Vlad the Impaler, from the band Drac and the Boyz! There's no shortage of weird rituals, superstitious peasants and wolves howling in the night with Vlad around. Awooooo!

Mostly C
Wowee! Nick Carter from Backstreet Boys is your secret Illuminati Master! He's a kind, giving kind of master, and we know you'll love the frequent trips to the mall for fresh new threads.

Mostly D
Great! You're slowly turning into a tree! Good luck with that, boo. You don't need a secret Illuminati Master in the woods.

Mostly E

Zounds! Your secret Illuminati master is all of Take That! Yep, the whole band. They're all working together to make your life super fun!

QUESTION CRESSIDA

THIS UNUSUAL LIFE! is highly delighted to bring you the wisdom of Cressida Flittersocks. In addition to bird watching and volcano registration, Cressida is a noted oracle and witch fancier from Northern Slimetown.

Please help Cressida,

My brother used my husband's sperm with a surrogate mother to have a child, wanting for our children to be actually related. I found out by accident, and the child is now 4. Should I demand that we get the child if anything happens to my brother instead of our deadbeat aunt, I mean they are my children's half-sibling?

Hela Outtaher

Dear Hela,

Matters of family are always deeply complicated when someone dies. If you were to insist that you're included in the will now, your brother will suspect that you're plotting to kill him in order to adopt his child. And obviously, you don't want him tipped off on this.

A simple concoction of lemons, lemon balm, lip balm and

dragon sugar in his tea will allow you to plant the idea without him necessarily noticing. It's a kind of tea-based inception process, and you can gently suggest the idea of willing the child to you instead of your aunt.

I would, however, advise you to have a serious conversation with both your husband and your brother. Your perception of how they perceive you may be altered by a little radical honesty. There's a reason your husband and brother didn't feel comfortable telling you about this five years ago, and you can all work through this together. You owe it to your children and your brother's child to reconcile and connect on the deepest level with the men and lizards in your life.

Dear Cressida,
I think my teenager is watching adult films. How can I stop her finding the films I'm in?
Fanny Adams

Dear Ms Adams,

You'd be surprised how often people come to me with this exact conundrum!

My advice is simply to be upfront with your teenager about your past career. Trust me, your teenager doesn't want to see you in those films any more than you want her to see you in them!

Instead, guide her towards some of the more niche genre of adult content you never participated in. Perhaps some of the historical recreation series, a little hang-gliding content or even something with furries?

This way you can sleep safe knowing she's exploring in a safe space, and who knows? Maybe something magical will awaken within her.

🕷

APRIL 1961

PRINCE LARKSPUR TO MARRY!

THAT'S RIGHT, we have official word from the Royal Palace that the heir to the throne, Prince Larkspur is to marry his sweetheart, Holly.

As you will recall, Miss Albert is a half fey, half human student of Rocksbridge university. She has recently graduated with a Bachelor of Business, focusing on the History of Fey Culture and Economics.

This Unusual Life! has learned the ceremony will take place in three full moon's time, when Holly will undertake the standard Trial of Worthiness. The trial is carried out according to ancient fey tradition. This magazine has heard that it will involve no less than three outfit changes, one battle with a minotaur and the carving of a staff from the old willow tree that grows in the palace.

Her most Illustrious Majesty Queen Laurel (may She ever rule our lands) will oversee the worthiness ceremony, which Holly must undertake totally alone. As tradition demands, Prince Larkspur will be chained nearby but unable to speak. This event will of course be televised and although some naysayers may hope that Holly fails, leaving our beauteous prince free to choose another spouse, we here at the magazine are rooting for Holly. She's an accomplished and efficient young lady, and we are confident that she cares enough for Larkspur to come through on top.

Mark your calendar for three full moons from now, and prep your watching party. This is going to be a night to remember!

- Cedric Ramekin reporting

FAMILY BBQ WITH A DIFFERENCE!

A WESTINSTON FAMILY had an unusual outdoor barbeque over the holiday weekend. The Abioye family, who have been experimenting with cooking in different environments, had invited several neighbours around for what they planned to be more than just a meal.

"We wanted to share something special with our friends," Malaika, mother of Mini said. Malaika and Mini live together in an ordinary Westinston cul-de-sac, and it had only been a few weeks earlier that Mini had discovered an unusual skill. Mini is, to the casual observer, a totally normal eleven-year-old. She's a competitive swimmer, a science fair winner and a part-time mermaid spotter.

"The neighbours all turned up with cornbread, jellied soda, bread rolls, salads, desserts and things to put on the grill," Malaika said. "It was a really beautiful day - just perfect for an outdoor meal. Once we were ready to fire up the barbeque, that's when Mini got to show off."

According to the neighbours in attendance, and several now viral videos taken at the time, Mini began by staring hard at the grill. "She moved into the middle of the group, quite close to the grill and just gazed at it," Malaika said. "It often needs a few moments to begin."

What happened next caused all in attendance to gasp. Mini ignited the barbeque with the power of her mind. "The kindling seemed to sing for a moment," says Terry, the Abioye's next door neighbour. "It was the strangest sound, very beautiful. I think, on reflection, it was the fire singing itself into being. It caught alight and Mini clapped her hands together over her head."

The barbeque, it goes without saying, was a huge success with many in attendance taking pictures and video of Mini setting fire to various things over the course of the night. "It was a real success," Malaika said. "And Mini's feeling really good about her powers now."

This wasn't always the case. Malaika went on to describe how, when Mini first manifested her pyrokinetic abilities a year ago, she was initially very afraid of them, and shy to show them off in public. "Honestly, I blame Frozen," Malaika says,"and the whole thing where the queen is afraid of her ice powers, I think Mini thought terrible things would happen to her. Having the community rally around her in this way has made a huge difference."

Pyrokinesis, or psychic fire control, is a very unusual skill and there are hardly any documented cases. Mini now sees it as nothing but another skill she can work on, along with swimming in a straight line and examining maps for the best places to locate mermaids.

Mini is one of a growing number of children hitting puberty and discovering strange powers. This Unusual Life! is planning a series highlighting the highlights and struggles of these special teens. We encourage our readers to come forward and share their stories if they have a family member or friend going through something similar.

Please refer to form Q in the addendum if you'd like to share the story of a tween developing strange powers

- Mallory Te Moana reporting

MY BILLIONAIRE WIFE STABBED ME AND LEFT FOR HER HOMEWORLD - MARS!

THEIR RELATIONSHIP STARTED like so many others. Aneesa Mallick was working her ordinary and not at all glamorous job - as a barista at a small Stonemoor café. "It was an ordinary day," Aneesa says, her eyes sparkling as she remembered happier times. "I'd fallen over a few times, mixed up some orders, but in a really cute way, and that's when she walked in. Absolutely gorgeous, in this black suit, and ugh! I fell over right on her feet. She helped me up and introduced herself. That's how I met Sidney."

Sidney, despite being a billionaire and a successful entrepreneur, maintained a low profile. Many would have expected to have heard of her, being as she was, so successful in the field of business. "She was always so private," Aneesa said. "I thought it was just because of the money, but actually she was hiding a bigger secret."

After a whirlwind romance, the two got married in a private ceremony. "She flew us out to a private Resort in the South Pacific, one of those islands, you know, that are all jungle and beach? It was a lovely day, everything came off perfectly and we promised ourselves to each other. She was so gorgeous, really tall and her shoulders were just like, the best shoulders you've ever seen. I wore a beachy white dress and she wore a beach casual tuxedo. The ceremony was beautiful, really special. Gay marriage wasn't legal on that island, but we sorted out the paperwork before we left home."

But the happy union wasn't to last, as Aneesa started to notice Sidney's secretive, and even controlling behaviour. "She got me to quit working, which I didn't mind too much, but she was always out. I got lonely," Aneesa says. Her manner becomes sadder, she avoids my eyes as she remembers. "I was alone in this big house, and it was a really nice house, but it was just me. I'd read, or go for walks. I didn't know what to do with myself. I missed my friends. Then everything changed when I got pregnant."

Although some would be confused by a lesbian couple becoming pregnant without any plans to, Aneesa wasn't concerned. "Sidney was very reassuring, and said that it happened to her all the time. I wasn't entirely sure what that meant, but she kept bringing me gifts and drawing me baths, so I didn't mind too much. I guess, in retrospect, I should've realised it was too many baths. *Too many.*"

Two months into the pregnancy, things took a dark turn. "One night I complained I was having cramps, and she pulled out this huge knife. I was terrified. But I'll never forget what she said to me. She said 'Nees, darling, I love you, but I have to take our young back to Mars. They won't survive here, and you won't survive there. Please, take the house, take all the things. My bank account is in your name, now. Don't think of us. I'm so sorry.'"

Then she stabbed me in the stomach, and I passed out. When I woke up there was a surgical scar on my stomach, and my sister was there, nursing me. I guess Sidney had made sure I'd be all right, and had called her in. I was totally clean, no pregnancy and all alone.

Aneesa tears up at this point, and we have to take a break from the interview, during which she shows me photos from the wedding. They look incredibly happy and I can see in the photos that Sidney's shoulders are really well shaped and she's very tall.

"I had no idea she felt that way, let alone that she wanted to return home. Honestly, I thought she was just an ordinary, incredibly sexy billionaire."

Aneesa is living happily in the mansion now. She has adopted several stray dogs and LGBTQIA youths in the area can use her spare rooms if they find themselves in need. "I want to give back a little, help out those in need, and try and prevent something happening to someone else, with another Martian," Aneesa says. Her expression is determined as she looks to the future. "I loved Sidney, but I have come to understand, she just used me to repopulate her own planet. All I can do, on this planet, is to give of my love, and share my story. And enjoy all these billions of dollars, I guess."

At the time of printing, several months after this interview, Aneesa has opened a number of education and support centres for Martian Repopulation Survivors. If you, or someone you know would like to get support, please use these numbers.

- Peachy Buncheeks reporting

(editor's note: a scratch lottery ticket was attached to this story. It has been scratched off and isn't a winning ticket.)

꙰

PRINCE LARKSPUR AND PRINCESS HOLLY'S HAPPY EVER AFTER

THE ROYAL WEDDING was certainly the event of the season! Princess Holly, her bruises and scars from the Trials of Worthiness still fresh on her face, nevertheless looked radiant in a gown fashioned from pure starshine.

Prince Larkspur was positively beaming himself, his garb that of the old Fey court, in homage to family tradition. The chafe marks from the chains he was restrained with during the Trial of Worthiness glowed a pleasant baby blue colour.

Her most Venerable Majesty Queen Laurel (may She ever rule our lands) presided over the ceremony in a gown of thousands of green geckos, accentuated by a stylish butterfly the size of a dinner plate, perched on her hair.

The turnout for the wedding included such nobles as Larkspur's sister Lily, Princess Bluebell of the Summer court and several fey that humans were not able to retain the memory of. But didn't they all look fantastic?

(editor's note: The image bulldog clipped to this article was an illustrated infographic of good flowers and herbs to plant to attract bees. It's quite charming.)

The most dramatic event of the ceremony was the interruption by Prince Forest, an ex-lover of Prince Larkspur's, who has been under a curse for some centuries. He strode up the aisle, his eyes burning with eldritch light and demanded that Larkspur look upon him once more and say to his face that he didn't love him.

"All hope is lost, for I don't love you," Prince Larkspur replied. Prince Forest held up his head and shook his mighty antlers.

"I deserve to be loved by someone who loves and cherishes me!" He cried, and then to the wonder of all gathered, the curse upon Prince Forest was broken. Small scraps of pink and silver light shed off Forest's body and he took a seat to watch the wedding, apparently quite pleased with himself.

After that interruption, the ceremony was brief, but very beautiful. Although Her most Illustrious Majesty Queen Laurel (may She ever rule our lands) did give the lovers a severe warning about what should happen if they ever attempt to assassinate her and ascend the throne, the mood was extremely joyous. In fact the pixie dust thrown over the happy couple was caught by the wind and distributed over most of the city. This had the effect of energising and compelling citizens to dance, drink and sing joyful melodies of love until well into the next night.

Congratulations to Larkspur and Holly from the entire staff of This Unusual Life!

- Cedric Ramekin reporting

ADVERTORIAL

SacriNu Home Blood Altar Repair Kits

SACRINU HOME BLOOD altar repair kits are perfect for the person on the go!

These kits come with everything you need, from stone-fastening superglue, salts from distant mountain quarries and some duct tape, all packaged up in a designer case of your choosing. With over a dozen exclusive SacriNu designs, ranging from beige to taupe, we're sure you'll find something that's perfect for you.

Your blood altar deserves a lot of respect, and without a SacriNu repair kit how can you possibly expect to keep the Elder Gods happy?

To get your SacriNu blood altar repair kit simply watch the moon at the exact right time. Then a SacriNu rep in your area will come to you!

QUESTION CRESSIDA

As ever, This Unusual Life! is loudly ecstatic to bring you Question Cressida. Cressida is a noted oracle's mother and witchfinder from the demon realm of Northern Slimetown.

WHAT. IS. BEHIND. ME.

My dear, sweet, angel.

The thing behind you is nothing more or less than your doppelganger, and it will remain there until you make eye contact with it. Once that happens well, it's up to you what happens next - as you know many advise to **kill your double,** but for me it's always been helpful to have another set of eyes and ears across things.

What I'd really like you to focus on is how you're coming across on social media. I know you mean well, and you want to share your experiences, but please be mindful of how you are doing this. Your use of the word 'obviously' and 'the only right way' when describing your blood rituals can come across and condescending to those who simply enjoy different methods. Remember that your way may work best for you, but it is not to everyone's taste.

And be sure to call your siblings, they miss you.
Yours in perpetuity
Cressida Flittersocks

ADDENDA

THE STAFF OF THIS UNUSUAL LIFE!

(EDITOR'S NOTE, this staff list was stuffed sideways into the shoebox, and slightly water stained. A series of Rorschach test cards fell out of the paper)

Rami Centaur graduated from the University of Tiny Stockings in Westghost. Is it pronounced Raymi or Rahmi? We simply don't know, and Rami isn't telling. And is he an actual centaur ? Yes he is

    Peachy Buncheeks - small, furry and dedicated to the pursuit of truth in all things.

    Cedric Ramekin - our dedicated Royals correspondent. He has been a devoted follower of the esteemed royal family ever since he was kidnapped to be a prized attendant to Prince Larkspur as a child.

    Mallory Te Moana - Mallory has been with the magazine since it first started several decades ago. She has not aged a day but she often complains "I'm too old for this shit."

    Tiger Smith is definitely not a Tiger wearing a trenchcoat and brown shoes. Now working in the mall.

    Periwinkle Candyfloss - Periwinkle has a PHD in Mechanical Journalism from Oxford University and sometimes turns people into toads.

Flotto Forebough (RIP) - we remember Flotto's easy going nature, their love of music and their brown shoes (missing). Many gifts have arrived at the This Unusual Life! offices for Flotto, and these have been passed to their favourite Korean pop band.

Minor Key Marshall - there is little that can be printed of Minor Key's past, suffice it to say Mx Marshall loves you all and wishes nothing but peace for your family.

Cressida Flittersocks - advice columnist, seeker of the truth, houser of small mice and demon seeker.

Valpy Bennet also works here, we guess.

※

FORM Q

My name:

Name of tween:

Tween's pronouns:

Tween's strange and unusual ability is:

Date you first noticed this ability:

Social security number:

Barcode number on back of Tween's neck:

Tween's favourite colour:

How many times they walk backwards each day:

Number of odd dreams that seem to have a prophetic or vision-like quality. *Some examples include dreams of mass gatherings of strangers chanting their name, the sight of the moon with a crack through the middle or unusual amounts of wolves in a dream.*

Does your tween have an especially close relationship with a family pet or wild birds? Please give details:

Best contact number:

Tween's last school report results:

RECIPE FOR BREADHOGS

Put water, oil, yeast and sugar into the bowl of your most expensive stand mixer. A cheaper model will not yield ye softe and fluffy rolls.

Rest for ten minutes, you're doing so well!

Add a little flour, a lot of salt and one ostrich egg into the yeast mixture using your hook hand, or the dough hook attachment on your stand mixer. Add the remaining flour gradually until the dough forms a smooth ball which is humming softly. If it begins to whistle you have over mixed it, and must perform a quick charm over it using whatever you know of fey magic.

Give the dough some time to work out the best tune, perhaps ten minutes or so. I recommend using this time to study the biology, and particularly the skeletal structure, of your favourite hedgehogs. Ten minutes should be just enough time.

Realise you should have already preheated the oven, and do that now, pretend like it was always on.

Divide the dough into five centimetre parts with a large sword, and begin to fashion your breadhogs. The pointy nose is a vital aspect of the look of the thing, but be careful not to overdo this. Too pointy a snout and your bread will become ferret like. Remember to include cute spines, either by pressing into the dough with the tines of a fork, or by sinking toothpicks into the dough in even rows.

Arrange your breadhogs on a large baking tray, brush the tops with melted butter and bake them for ten minutes. During this time, have a quick shower and make sure to moisturise afterwards. Your skin is too valuable to let it dry out and the weather has been so harsh lately.

Once the breadhogs are golden brown, springy to touch, and ready to enrol in college, remove them from the oven and allow to cool before serving.

You may enjoy breadhogs alone with Netflix or invite friends to join you.

THANKS

Thanks to Ellen Boucher, for being my sounding board throughout a lot of this project, your insights and ideas were invaluable.

Thanks also to my beta readers, Liz and Kitty for not saying no when I asked you to look over this truly unusual project and for giving me great feedback.

Thanks to Spike Milligan, Jim Henson and all the Muppet Show writers, Roald Dahl, Shel Silverstein and all the authors I read as a kid who instilled a true love for nonsense in me. Without your books, none of this could have happened. And for that I am also deeply sorry. More recently thanks also to Neil Gaiman, Joseph Fink and Jeffrey Cranor.

To my spouse, I love you as Prince Larkspur loves Holly but with a lot less violence.

. . .

This book is a compilation of a project I published first on Patreon, with some exciting editions and a fair bit of editing presented here. It's kind of what happens when I listen to my dreams and let my subconscious run wild. I hope you enjoyed it!

Busy now

A witch in the broom closet probably shouldn't be so interested in a ghost hunter, right?

That Basil is a librarian comes as no surprise to his Mt Eden community. That he's a witch? Yeah. That might raise more than a few eyebrows.

When Sebastian, a paranormal investigator filming a web series starts snooping around Basil's library, he stirs up more than just Basil's heart.

Between Basil's own self-doubt, a ghost who steals books and Sebastian, an enthusiastic extrovert bent on uncovering secrets, Basil's life is about to get a lot more complicated.

Overdues and Occultism is a sweet, no heat contemporary novella about a witch living in Auckland, New Zealand. MM romance, HEA.

You can read a follow up about the same characters in Jingle Spells, the Witchy Fiction Christmas anthology

ALSO BY JAMIE SANDS

The Suburban Book of the Dead

A Young Adult ghost story

The Other Side of the Mirror

A queer urban fantasy mystery set in Auckland, New Zealand

Honeymoon in Japan

A travel journal of a month's trip around Japan

ALSO PUBLISHED BY GREY KELPIE STUDIO

Rival Princes by Jaxon Knight

Buy now

There are three golden rules for new recruits at Fairyland Theme Park:

1. No breaking character, even if you're dying of heat exhaustion
   2. Always give guests the most magical time
   3. No falling in love.

Nate's only been at work one day, and he's already broken all three.

Fast-tracked into a Prince role, Nate's at odds with Dash, the handsome not-so-charming prince who is supposed to be training him. Nate doesn't know how he ended up on Dash's bad side, but the broody prince sure is hot when he gets mad.

Dash has worked long and hard to play Prince Justice at Fairyland. Now, instead of focusing on his own performance, he is forced to train newbie Nate to be the perfect prince. Nate's annoying ease with the guests coupled with his charm and good looks could dethrone Dash from his number one spot … so why does he secretly want to kiss him?

Fairyland heats up as sparks fly between the two rival princes. Will they get their fairytale romance before they're kicked out of Fairyland for good?

Find out in this standalone MM contemporary romance by Jaxon Knight, set in an amusement park where fairytales can come true.

ALSO PUBLISHED BY GREY KELPIE STUDIO

Recipe for Chaos by Jaxon Knight

Buy now

The recipe is simple:
  Charlie cooks an amazing meal
  Charlie impresses heir to the theme park Max Jones
  Charlie gets a promotion and a dash of control over his kitchen

But the perfect recipe becomes unpalatable with one wrong ingredient and Max Jones is not behaving how Charlie expected…

Max is meant to inherit the entire Fairyland theme park but he just wants to party, have fun and bed as many people as possible. That is, until he meets Charlie and falls for him so hard he can't even finish the delicious meal.

Charlie doesn't have time for clubs or helicopter flights over the city, but Max is accustomed to getting what he wants, and he wants Charlie.

Featuring one part Billionaire, one part sensible chef, six cups of attraction, a generous dose of snark and a freshly prepared Happy Ever After.

ALSO PUBLISHED BY GREY KELPIE STUDIO

The Good, the Bad and the Dad by Jaxon Knight

Buy now

Haru is a single dad, a widower, doing his best to balance his career and raising his little girl, Minako. Thankfully Fairyland theme park is a haven for both of them. However, when both a prince and a pirate start courting Haru, his balancing act gets a lot harder...

Cillian plays a pirate at Fairyland theme park and he loves playing the roguish character in and out of work hours. The last thing he wants is to settle down with a guy with a kid, so can't he stop thinking about handsome single dad Haru. And why can't he stop looking at pictures of Prince Magnificence and his stupid symmetrical face? And why does he keep running into both of them?

Grayson feels he's found his home in the role of Prince Magnificence, but he's more likely to run from love than seek it out. Until he meets Haru, that is. Christmas is complicated by Grayson's role being featured in a special Christmas celebration. Not only that, but his feelings for Haru, and his possible rival Cillian keep on growing. Maybe it's time to stop hiding who he really is?

The Good, the Bad and the Dad is a sweet MMM romance featuring a single father, a rogue and a trans prince with a heart of gold. No cheating, just the tentative first steps into polyamory.

ALSO PUBLISHED BY GREY KELPIE STUDIO

Tailor Made Christmas by Jaxon Knight

Buy Now

Sparks fly and old hurts flare as two men too afraid of their feelings discover some things can't be buried.

Teddy loves his job working in the Wardrobe department of a theme park, but his love life needs resuscitation. The last thing he expected was his high school best friend and crush walking in to be fitted for a prince costume.

Art wants to make it big in Hollywood, and getting a job as a handsome prince might not seem like the obvious first step, but if the rumors are true it could be the break he needs. Instead, he comes face to face with Teddy, the one he left behind.

Tailor Made Chirstmas is a sweet second chance romance with queer characters, set in a fairy tale themed amusement park. Guaranteed HEA. Some cursing, no cheating. This is a shorter length novella style book

ALSO PUBLISHED BY GREY KELPIE STUDIO
The Trouble With Order by Jaxon Knight

Buy Now

Opposites attract, right?

Link's past was difficult but he learned to skim through life and have things work out right, Teayang has worked for what he has and sacrificed things along the way.

When Taeyang is cast as Lord Order, the villain opposite Link's fun-loving Fairy Mischief, there's instant chemistry that can't be denied.

Outside of acting at Fairyland, Link's life is falling apart and he has no idea how to handle it alone. But years of putting up walls and projecting a happy image makes it impossible to ask for help as well.

Taeyang may love playing a villain, but in real life, he yearns to reach out to his acting partner, if he'd only accept that help...

Can a villain become a friend? Or something even more?

www.ingramcontent.com/pod-product-compliance
Lightning Source LLC
Chambersburg PA
CBHW022127170626
46808CB00002B/882